Robert G. Barrett was raised in Sydney's Bondi where he worked mainly as a butcher. After thirty years he moved to Terrigal on the Central Coast of New South Wales. Robert has appeared in a number of films and TV commercials but prefers to concentrate on a career as a writer. He is the author of twenty-two books, including *Goodoo Goodoo*, *Leaving Bondi*, *The Ultimate Aphrodisiac*, *Mystery Bay Blues*, *Rosa-Marie's Baby*, *Crime Scene Cessnock* and *The Tesla Legacy*.

To find out more about Bob and his books
visit these websites:
www.robertgbarrett.com.au
or
www.harpercollins.com.au/robertgbarrett

Also by Robert G. Barrett
and published by HarperCollins:

So What Do You Reckon?

Mud Crab Boogie

Goodoo Goodoo

The Wind and the Monkey

Leaving Bondi

The Ultimate Aphrodisiac

Mystery Bay Blues

Rosa-Marie's Baby

Crime Scene Cessnock

The Tesla Legacy

LES NORTON
AND THE
CASE OF THE
TALKING PIE
CRUST

ROBERT G. BARRETT

HarperCollins*Publishers*

HarperCollins*Publishers*

First published in Australia in 2007
by HarperCollins*Publishers* Australia Pty Limited
ABN 36 009 913 517
www.harpercollins.com.au

HarperCollins*Publishers*
25 Ryde Road, Pymble, Sydney NSW 2073, Australia
31 View Road, Glenfield, Auckland 10, New Zealand
77–85 Fulham Palace Road, London W6 8JB, United Kingdom
2 Bloor Street East, 20th floor, Toronto, Ontario M4W 1A8, Canada
10 East 53rd Street, New York NY 10022, USA

National Library of Australia Cataloguing-in-Publication data:

Barrett, Robert G.
  The case of the talking pie crust.
  ISBN 978 0 7322 8396 4 (pbk.).
  I. Title.
A823.3

Cover design by Matt Stanton, HarperCollins Design Studio
Cover images: Hieroglyphic images courtesy of Shutterstock; tarot illustrations by Matt Stanton;
Gravy Pie illustration by Emile Mercier, from his book of illustrations, *Gravy Pie.*
Internal illustration by Emile Mercier, from his book of illustrations, *Gravy Pie.*
Author photo: Sarhn McArthur Photography
Typeset in 12/20pt Minion by Helen Beard, ECJ Australia Pty Limited
Printed and bound in Australia by Griffin Press
70gsm Bulky Book Ivory used by HarperCollins*Publishers* is a natural, recyclable product made
from wood grown in sustainable forests. The manufacturing processes conform to the
environmental regulations in the country of origin, Finland.

5 4 3 2 1   07 08 09 10

THIS BOOK IS DEDICATED
TO GEORGE BURRARRAWANGA
AND THE WARUMPI BAND

A MESSAGE FROM THE AUTHOR

Of all the diversions in life, there is none so proper to fill up its empty spaces as the reading of useful and entertaining authors.

Joseph Addison, 1672–1719, English essayist, poet, playwright and statesman.

There you go. If you haven't got the brains to come up with something yourself, you can always do a little literary shoplifting and plagiarise somebody else. Not that I'm claiming to be a useful and entertaining author. But I manage to sell a few books and I reckon that's a pretty good quote.

Anyway, once again I have to apologise to all the people who have written to me and are waiting on a reply. As usual, I've got letters up my Goolwah, but I'm doing my best to answer them. So with a bit of luck, you should get a reply. Although some letters do get lost. The same goes to members of my captive audience wanting books for the gaol libraries. I'm doing my best there, too.

Now, to this book. The reason I dedicated it to George Burrarrawanga and the Warumpi Band is because I like their music and like to put it in my books. 'Blackfella/Whitefella', 'My Island Home' and 'Jailanguru Pakarnu' are classic Australian songs. Also, a big Aborigine friend of mine was in Broome and he bumped into the Warumpi Band. They liked their music getting a mention in my books and sent me one signed by every member of the band. I was absolutely rapt. I've signed a heap of books, but I reckon that would be the only time an author has got back one of his books signed by his readers. So I dedicated the book to George and the boys in appreciation of a kind thought and some great music. Sadly George Burrarrawanga is not with us any more and the band has broken up. Let's hope they get back together again and give us some more good music.

Okay, the book itself. I have to admit, you couldn't find a more stupid name for a book than *The Case of the Talking Pie Crust*. It's ridiculous. But once you've read the book you'll see that it makes sense. However, to get into the guts of things, you have to find out about Emile Mercier. Emile was an incisive humourist with a zany sense of humour and his old cartoons and comics were insane. No one knows a great deal about him. But try and find his works in your local library or on the net. I'm sure you'll agree.

The cave full of Egyptian carvings is the real deal. It's out in the middle of nowhere and is one of the weirdest things I've ever seen. I put some photos and more information up on my website. The photos aren't the best, but they'll give you an idea of what's going on.

I might add, I'm in this book, too. I've always wanted a guernsey in a Robert G. Barrett book, so I gave myself a cameo role as one of the characters. I'm stoked. If you still can't find me, there's some photos of this particular scene on my website as well. There's also photos from *The Tesla Legacy* tour and a recent speakers gig I did for the libraries in Cairns. One photo of me roaring drunk on margaritas with my face looking like an eggplant is worth the price of a mouse click on its own. I also want to say hello to the men and women in our armed services, wherever they might be. I know I've got a big following in the military, my books remind them of home, and I've been swapping parcels of books for T-shirts. Some of the T-shirts they sent me back from Afghanistan are unreal. Our serving men and women do a great job and Australia a great service and we should all be proud of them.

Well, that's about it for the time being. I'm not sure what my next book will be all about, though I'm thinking of sending Les over to Western Australia. I'd like to set a story between Perth, Broome and Derby. Any sand gropers out there got any stories or ideas, drop me a line. There might even be a drink in it for you. In the meantime, thanks for all your support and letters. I truly appreciate it. And I'll no doubt get to meet and greet some of you when I'm doing book signings for *Les Norton and the Case of the Talking Pie Crust.*

All the best,

Robert G. Barrett

LES NORTON
AND THE
CASE OF THE
TALKING PIE
CRUST

Sprawled comfortably on his backyard banana chair in a plain white T-shirt over an old pair of blue shorts, Norton smiled and shook his head in admiration as the CD in the ghetto blaster alongside him cut out. How can a couple of blokes as old as those two keep pumping out filthy, foot-stomping rock 'n roll as mean as that? he asked himself. Christ! Buddy Guy has to be pushing eighty. Jerry Lee Lewis is in his seventies. And they're still making hacks out of musicians half their age.

Norton had been listening to a CD called *Last Man Standing*, featuring Jerry Lee Lewis doing duos with everyone from Jimmy Page to Neil Young to Mick Jagger. The particular track that had Norton shaking his head was called 'Halicol Boogie', in which the crusty old Southern rocker pumped out a scorching rock 'n roll duo with veteran bluesman Buddy Guy.

'Why'd they call it Halicol?' asked Buddy Guy, when the track ended.

'Halicol it something,' replied Jerry Lee.

Norton liked the CD that much, he put down his cup of lemongrass tea with ginger, reached lazily across and played it again.

It was mid-morning on a delightful, autumn Saturday in beautiful downtown Bondi and a light sou'wester was pushing a scattering of puffy clouds towards the ocean, while the languidly rising sun warmed the day. Normally at this time, Les would be getting out of bed after a hard day's night at the pickle factory instead of lying out in the backyard alone, catching some rays and getting into a bit of boogie. But the big Queenslander had been cruelly laid low by a virus he'd picked up at the Kelly Club and had to take a week off work. The bug hit him Saturday night when he suddenly started sneezing and his nose began running. By Sunday he felt absolutely rooted. Monday he was still sneezing and coughing up what looked like pineapple yoghurt, so he rang Price to painfully inform the dapper, grey-haired casino owner he was at death's door and about to see a doctor. Stick the Kelly Club in his arse and get someone else in for the rest of the week. That was no problem. Billy Dunne's cousin Royce was in need of a dollar and only too willing to help out. So Les set off to see a good doctor he knew up in Old South Head Road, who prescribed him some industrial-strength antibiotics along with some good advice. Les got his prescription filled, then drove home, gobbled down the antibiotics with several vitamin C tablets and honey and lemon, then crawled miserably into bed to have a good sulk and sweat out the evil spirits.

Whatever pills the good doctor prescribed certainly worked. By Wednesday, Les had stopped coughing and sneezing. By

Thursday he was on his feet. Friday he had a slow jog along the soft sand on Bondi Beach and on Saturday morning after a good night's sleep, Les was smiling and fit for work. However, Les decided to keep this to himself and have a few more days off. So he rang Billy's wife earlier to say he was still pretty crook and tell Billy to keep his cousin at the club till the end of the following week. Lyndy said she'd pass the message on and would he like her to bring him round some chicken soup? That was quite all right thanks, Les lied to her, as he glanced at the empty plate in front of him, which a short time ago had been piled with scrambled eggs. He still hadn't quite got his appetite back. After hanging up, Les sorted things out in the backyard, relaxed in his banana chair and mulled things over while he sipped his herb tea. And as the sun rose and the music played the general consensus was — apart from an untimely spell flat on his back — life was all right.

His brief sojourn at the health farm had done him the world of good and Les was pleased with himself for not outing the murderer. He put the ignominy of being date-raped behind him and rang Estelle the girl from Leichhardt. But she was going one way and Les was working nights and going another. However, they both swore to meet up for dinner and a movie one evening.

Les also tried to maintain a healthier lifestyle now when it came to food. Although his appetite hadn't diminished one iota, he was eating more salads and vegetables than before and laying off the junk food. If he wanted to snack, Les would eat nourishing sandwiches. His favourite was grated carrot and cheese, topped with lettuce and slices of Spanish onion, on wholemeal bread spread with Promite. He still liked chocolates and maybe a pizza marinara if the occasion arose and was also extremely partial to date smoothies. Clover put him onto them and her secret was to soak the seedless dates in hot water till they softened, before dropping them into a blender and adding full-cream milk. The only problem was, one date smoothie had enough calories in it to send a rocket to Jupiter. Add a banana and a scoop of ice cream and you could send the rocket into another solar system. But Les figured you had to allow yourself certain indulgences. Another was coffee.

Caffeine withdrawls, caffeine poisoning, caffeine addiction. It didn't matter. Les still enjoyed good strong coffee. He'd tried decafs, Bambu and other ersatz blends. But apart from tea and one particular herb type, Les wouldn't have given the rest to a Jap on Anzac Day. Coffee was coffee. Slaves had died for coffee, dictatorships had fallen because of coffee, duels had been fought over coffee. SBS did three-part documentaries about coffee. Coffee was more than a beverage. Coffee drinking was a major social event. And if there was anywhere better to socialise with people over coffee than Bondi, Les wasn't aware of it. There was a coffee shop with chairs and tables spread across the footpath on every corner. In Hall Street, or Halal Street, as Norton's Jewish mate, Benny the Beak, liked to call it, coffee shops were cheek by jowl. Plus the Bondi coffee shops were more than that. They were scenes. Scenes brimming with would-be scriptwriters, actors, authors, poets, film directors or whatever, all propped in front of their laptops looking pensive and intense while they gossiped about the arts and stabbed each other in the back. And the various scenes were like armed camps. The mob at Enzo's didn't like the team at Gemini's, who despised the punters at Sardana's, who loathed the rabble at Vivace's. It was more delicious than the coffee. And strolling amongst it all, acting the epitome of elegant sophistication and sagacious perspicacity while he got his caffeine hits and grooved on the pettifoggery and intrigues, was Norton.

On the subject of strolling, or getting around town in general, Les had recently been doing a bit of soul-searching. Did he really need his Holden Berlina? It still went okay. But someone had side-swiped it while he was at work, he'd backed into a shopping trolley bay at Bondi Junction, and a brief hailstorm hadn't helped the duco. And for some reason, the smell from the previous owner's corpse was wafting back through the interior on hot humid days like a curried egg fart. Parking and traffic in the Eastern Suburbs was a horror show; all you did was drive from one set of lights to another and wait. Petrol wasn't cheap and Les didn't have a family. What use was a spacious four-seater, six-cylinder car? Avid environmentalist Spike Milligan had espoused driving the smallest car possible and for a crazy old Goon, he made a lot of sense.

Les had been thinking along the lines of a secondhand Mini Cabriolet. But the car that caught his eye was a thief-proof hybrid number a German company was bringing out, that ran on the smell of an oil rag and looked like something out of Tomorrow Land. Plus it had a heap of room inside, loads of extras and you could park it almost anywhere. The only blue was, they were around seventy-five thousand dollars on the road. Les could have dug that up out of the backyard, and he was sorely tempted. But it was a lot of money to fork out for a glorified tin box on wheels only to find out later you didn't like the thing. But if a lazy earn close to that amount fell in out of nowhere, Les would have dug up the shortfall and had a talk to a dealer.

Norton did make one momentous purchase. He finally stepped into the twenty-first century and bought himself a mobile phone. Reluctant to the last. The final straw arrived one shitty night when the Berlina died coming home from the Kelly Club and Les had to trudge around Edgecliff in the rain, searching for a phone box to ring the NRMA. All the phone boxes were vandalised, so Les threw the towel in and hailed a passing taxi to take him home. When he returned to his car the following day, he'd been pinched for parking and his hubcaps were gone. The minute the NRMA mechanic revived the Berlina, Les went straight to the nearest Telstra outlet and bought an LG something or other that played music, tuned into Foxtel, took photos and had a range of other functions Les wasn't interested in. All Norton knew was, he could ring the NRMA or whoever and people could ring him.

However, Les wasn't sure if his new mobile was a blessing or a curse. Everybody at work had his number and he'd got drunk at a couple of soirees and given it to people who had handed it on to other people. Now he had uncertain women and blokes he hardly knew ringing him out of the blue wanting to talk absolute

Edgar. Since the novelty faded, Les would have preferred to keep the thing switched off. But Price advised him to leave it on in case there was an emergency. Though Les had a feeling Price mostly liked to ring him up from the races, when he had one or two Dimple Haighs under his belt and he'd just given some poor unfortunate bookmaker a kicking.

Mobile phones aside, Les had the house to himself this particular Saturday morning, because Warren had stayed the night at his new girlfriend's place. His old girlfriend Clover's glassware company had offered her a twelve-month overseas posting in Genova, Italy. With the posting went a raise, an expense account and a fully furnished apartment, making it virtually a free trip to see Europe and come back with money in the bank. And although it broke Clover's heart to leave Warren and Warren's to be without Clover, she would have been mad not to take it. Les drove them to the airport, where they joined Clover's friends and family and he was standing right next to Warren and Clover when they tearfully kissed each other goodbye, before Clover jetted off business class to Rome, flying Air Italia. However, despite all the tears and sorrow, it wasn't long before Warren met Beatrice. A Hunters Hill girl who ran a small screen-printing business at Waterloo, where she lived above the premises.

Beatrice was in her late twenties and comfortably built, with wide, red lips set in a square face, and wore glasses under a mane of long, black hair cut in a fringe. Beatrice had a nice nature, but Les churlishly nicknamed her Ugly Betty and was a little indifferent towards her for no other reason than he liked

Clover, and felt Warren could have waited a little longer before he let her lease expire. But it was none of Norton's business and he imagined if Clover met some good-looking Italian count with a red Ferrari and plenty of lira to toss around, she wouldn't stay lonely too long herself. Les did find one thing interesting about Beatrice. She was a conversant numismatologist and made money on the side buying and selling coins through the internet. Name an Australian coin and Beatrice could tell you where it was minted and how many there were in circulation. Beatrice also allowed her sideline to influence her dress sense and often wore a pair of earrings made from two 1910 threepences, plus she had a twenty-four carat gold necklace with a gold sovereign for a pendant. Beatrice liked Les and his tough guy persona and gave him a pinky ring with a 1938 sixpence in it. Les appreciated Ugly Betty's gift. But sadly, the sixpenny coin finished up embedded in the forehead of a big Islander who tried to king hit Billy outside the Kelly Club when Billy wasn't looking. Les apologised to Beatrice and said it came off when he was changing a flat tyre and rolled down a drain. Beatrice said that was okay, she'd find him another one.

Les was listening to Jerry Lee Lewis doing a great duo with Neil Young and watching a little butcher bird that was watching a little skink lizard near the fence, and was about to advise the skink to take it on the toe when the phone rang inside. Norton closed his eyes and thought, Now this is when I should have my mobile next to me. So I don't have to get up off my big fat arse.

He tossed the remains of his tea towards the unsuspecting skink to scare it away, then walked into the loungeroom and picked up the phone.

'Hello?'

'What are you doing, Shitbags?'

'What am I doing, Warren?' replied Les. 'Well, I was sitting out in the backyard taking it easy, until you rang and fucked everything up.'

'Shit! I'm sorry.'

'Yeah, I'll bet,' grunted Norton. 'So where are you? Over at your concubine's place, I imagine.'

'Please don't call her that,' said Warren. 'She's my lady.'

'Lady? Ohh don't give me the Edgar Britts,' snorted Les. 'She's either your girlfriend or your sheila. Don't give me this fuckin lady shit, you imposter.'

'Jesus you're a fuckin nark.'

'I know. It comes from putting up with you. So you're over at Ugly Betty's.'

'And don't call her that either,' corrected Warren. 'It's Beatrice.'

'Holy shit! Beatrice, Beetroot. Beatrix bloody Potter. Fair dinkum, Warren. What the fuck do you want? This is one of the nicest Saturday mornings I've had to myself in ages and you have to stuff things up. Fuck you. Piss off.'

'Okay,' said Warren. 'If that's the way you want to be, you miserable big prick. In your arse. I was going to offer you an earn.'

'An earn?' Norton's ears pricked up. 'Keep talking, Woz.'

'Yeah. I knew that'd make you change your tune, you tight-arsed cunt. All right. How would you like a chance to make fifty thousand bucks?'

'Fifty grand!' exclaimed Norton. 'Warren. My friend and confidante. What do I have to do? A nice TV commercial. Do you want me to promote Versace or Armani's latest range? Does Russell Crowe want me to run on for Souths? I still follow the Roosters. But I can soon switch to the red and green. No problems. Go the mighty Rabbitohs.'

'No. Nothing like that,' replied Warren. 'You know Bodene Menjou.'

Les thought for a moment. 'Yeah. Yeah, Menny Menjou. I did him a favour once and he slipped me a nice earn. He's Albanian.'

'That's right,' said Warren.

'He's a shifty cunt. I know that.'

'Agreed,' replied Warren. 'Anyway. He's had a film script knocked off.'

'A film script?' said Les. 'I didn't know Menny was into movies.'

'Neither did I,' answered Warren. 'But I was having a drink with Beatrice at one of the local fleshpots last night and he, happened to be there. I got talking to him. And he's quietly offering fifty grand if anyone can find his missing film script. He specifically asked that I mention this to you. He thinks you're a super sleuth and you might be able to find it for him.'

'Does he now,' smiled Les. 'Okey doke, Woz. For that sort of money, I'm interested. What do I have to do?'

'Right. I'll give you his mobile number,' said Warren. 'But rather than ring him, he'll be down Azulejos at Seven Ways this morning. He'd like to meet you there. You know it?'

'Azulejos? Yeah. It's a scene near the Rex. I can walk down in five minutes.'

'Okay. You got a Biro?'

'I sure have.' Les picked up a Biro alongside a notepad on the phone table. 'Righto Woz, me old mate. Fire away.'

Les wrote down the phone number then read it back to Warren. 'Okay Woz. That sounds kosher. And he's down there waiting for me?'

'Yep. He'll probably be with his girlfriend.'

'Barbara Beauty Spot? Are they still an item?'

'He was with her last night.'

'Ain't love grand. So what's your story, Woz?' Les asked.

'I'll be home later to pick up some clothes,' replied Warren. 'Then I'm off to Surfers Paradise to shoot a promo for the Grand Prix. I'm taking Beatrice and we probably won't be back till Friday.'

'Okay. You want a lift to the airport?'

'No. It's all arranged.' Warren blew into a hanky at the other end of the line. 'Shit! I just hope I'm not coming down with that same wog you had.'

'I doubt if you got if off me, Woz,' said Les. 'I've been quarantined in my room all week.'

'I doubt it, too,' answered Warren. 'You wouldn't even give that away, you miserable arse. All right, Horrible. I might see you this arvo.'

'Okay mate. See you then.'

Les put the phone down then walked back outside and turned off the ghetto blaster. After a quick glance at his watch, he strolled into the kitchen, poured himself a glass of mineral water from the fridge, then took it into the loungeroom and sat down to have a think about Bodene Menjou.

Like a lot of other shifties around the Eastern Suburbs, Les knew him from the Kelly Club. A good card player who seemed to win more times than he lost, Menjou was a beefy, black-haired man around forty, who wore thick-rimmed glasses and always reminded Les and Billy of Ronnie Kray, one of the notorious London gangsters the Kray Twins. The resemblance was that close, the boys would often take the piss when he showed up at the club and put on cockney accents. Like Ronnie Kray, Bodene didn't waste any smiles and was always in the company of one or two equally dour heavies. But if Menny had links to the Albanian Mafia, they were the most ruthless, violent criminals in the world. Even the Italian Mafia and the Chinese Triads based in London feared them and did nothing when they encroached into their rackets. They were into drug dealing and such, but their main sources of illegal income were prostitution and people smuggling, from which they made millions. Les wasn't quite sure what Menny's rort was. But not far from Norton's house in Bondi, Menny ran a pizza shop called the Lushnje 33, situated amongst a small cluster of shops on the way to Bellevue Hill. Les pulled up to sample the pizzas late one afternoon and noticed a bloke walk out of Menny's shop with two takeaway coffees, which he casually tossed to a friend waiting in a car outside, who just as casually tossed them onto the back seat. Les figured the coffee either came in a new, completely spill-proof type of container, or it was as thick as tar, and decided to get a pizza somewhere else.

Bodene owned an immaculate old British racing green MG that got stolen around Christmas one year, sending the Albanian gangster slightly ballistic. Bodene loved his vintage MG and one night at the club he told Les of his bad luck, and if Les, who knew a lot of people, happened upon the perpetrators of this foul deed, there was a nice drink in it for him. Les wasn't all that interested. But said he'd see what he could do.

Not long afterwards, Les was having a solo jog around the back streets of Bondi, burning up a lazy hour before lunch. He was jogging down Glenayr Lane, not far from Azulejos, when he noticed a garage with the roller door partially open. MGs are built close to the ground and Les got a glimpse of green. He knelt down to take a look under the shutter and sure enough, there was Menny's vintage MG. Later that day Les strolled up to the Lushnje 33 and gave Bodene an enthralling line of bullshit, about how at great expense and after a lengthy investigation that involved asking people from everywhere and all walks of life, he'd managed to find his missing MG. He gave Menny the details then left him to it. Later that evening, as Les was getting ready for work, Bodene called round Chez Norton, thanked Les and slipped him five thousand dollars. Les hid the money in his room and drove to the club, keeping what happened to himself. The following day, Les was having a coffee with the morning paper and on page three was an article. A house in Glenayr Lane Bondi had burned down and two bodies had been recovered. Les never mentioned this to Menny when he eventually showed up at the club and Menny never gave Les so much as a second look. But after that, Menny was very friendly towards Les and showed him a lot of respect.

Les finished his water and stared into the empty glass. Well, if I'm fartarsing around with the Albanian Mafia, I'd better fartarse around very carefully, he thought. Not that I can see myself getting into too much trouble looking for a missing film script. It's not like a suitcase full of dope or a box of machine guns. And finding it won't be like fluking a car sitting in a garage. But, concluded Les, for fifty grand it's certainly worth having a look around and asking a few questions.

Les stood up and took his empty glass out to the kitchen, then changed into a clean grey T-shirt with CANADIAN PANORAMA on the front, a pair of blue cargoes and his Balance trainers. Five minutes later he'd locked the house, and after adjusting his sunglasses under a white baseball cap, was strolling down Cox Avenue towards the corner of Hall Street and Glenayr Avenue with his mobile phone stuffed in a side pocket of his cargoes.

Hall Street was buzzing when Les crossed over into Glenayr Avenue, and by the time he reached Curlewis Street, he'd passed half-a-dozen coffee shops packed with the local café society.

Further down he could see the shops at Seven Ways, and on the Warners Avenue corner was Azulejos.

Les had only ever been in there a couple of times. Originally, it was an old butcher's shop and still had the rough, patchy yellow concrete floor, glass showcase and meat rails hanging from the ceiling. There was a magazine rack on the left when you walked in, alongside shelves of organic and imported food, and high up in an opposite corner, looking down on the chairs and tables, were two framed posters Les would have loved to have had in his loungeroom: a Muslim woman with an AK-47, and a North Vietnamese girl cradling an MAT-49. The café still had the large bay windows and the doorway faced a small park, where two gum trees edged by sandstone blocks took pride of place. There were chairs and tables on the footpath and people would sit around under the trees, often on their own fold-up chairs. An empty shop stood next door and alongside that was an old shop that sold recycled designer clothes. Further round was another al fresco style restaurant, the Sonata.

Azulejos appeared to be thriving when Les reached the corner of Warners Avenue and punters were either standing around or filling the chairs and tables in or outside the café. At the same time, the council was ripping up the road and had most of the area cordoned off; a concrete truck was pouring slurry, there were workers in green fluoro vests everywhere and a young girl from the council was frantically running around amongst the noise and confusion with a STOP and GO sign trying to divert the impatient Saturday morning traffic. Les ducked between the girl

15

with the STOP and GO sign and a VW Golf and started to cross the road. As he did, he spotted Bodene with a man and two women, all sitting beneath the trees in fold-up chairs, next to two shiny Harley Davidsons. One of the women was Bodene's girlfriend, Barbara Beauty Spot.

Barbara's surname was Lewis and she got the nickname Beauty Spot because she had a mole on her neck shaped like a pineapple. She had worked at the Kelly Club prior to leaving for London, where she got nicked for fraud and did a year in a women's prison before they deported her back to Australia. Back home, she got into modelling and a little acting and somehow finished up with Bodene. Barbara was likeable enough and honest when she worked at the club. But she wasn't over-endowed with smarts and no one had been surprised when Beauty Spot got busted with a stack of forged traveller's cheques.

As he got closer, Les checked out Bodene and his party. Menjou was wearing a pair of dark slacks, a black polo shirt and oxblood loafers, and Barbara seated on his left, looked relaxed in a denim skirt and red top, her blonde hair stacked on top of her head. The girl on Barbara's left, wearing a lacy pink V-neck top over a pair of white jeans, was an attractive green-eyed brunette and had fox written all over her. And seated on Menny's right, the Slavic-featured man, wearing a pair of shin-length black shorts and a black and white checked shirt, was a monster, with a jaw like an iron gate and a big domed forehead beneath a crop of thick black hair. The way he was crammed into the fold-up chair made it look as if it was ready to collapse under him in a pile of torn canvas and twisted metal. Les couldn't remember seeing the bloke before, but he felt he'd seen the girl somewhere.

Menny looked up as Les appeared in front of them and an unusually warm smile spread across his face. 'Les, my good friend,' he said, standing up and offering his hand. 'Thank you for coming down.'

Les shook Bodene's hand. 'That's okay, Menny,' he replied.

'And how are you?'

'I'm good, thanks Menny. How's yourself?'

Bodene gestured. 'How is it, you Aussies say? Wouldn't be dead for quids?'

'That's good, mate,' smiled Norton.

'Les. You know Barbara.'

'Yeah. How are you, Barbara?'

'Fine, thanks Les,' nodded Barbara. 'And this is Topaz.'

Les offered the other girl his hand. 'Hello, Topaz. How are you?'

Topaz shook Norton's hand and gave him a very heavy once up and down from behind a pair of cool, green eyes. 'I'm really good, thank you, Les. What about yourself?' she purred.

Les nodded to Menny. 'Like Bodene said. Wouldn't be dead for quids.'

'And this is Lasjoz.'

The big man lumbered to his feet and Norton barely came up to his chin. 'Hullo Les,' he said in a friendly growl as he offered his hand. 'Bodene tells me many things about you.'

'All good I would imagine,' smiled Les, shaking the big man's hand. 'Nice to meet you, Lasjoz.' Les noticed a couple in black berets and sunglasses getting up from a table in front of the restaurant. 'I'll grab a seat.'

Les picked up a chair and sat down in front of Bodene as Lasjoz squeezed himself back into his. At the same time, a dark-haired waitress walked over in a pair of black jeans and a white T-shirt with a piccaninny's face on the front saying BUCKWHEAT.

'Can I get you something else?' the waitress asked, picking up their empty cups.

'Yes. The same again,' said Bodene. 'Les?'

'Yeah. I'll just have an Al Pacino thanks.'

'No problem,' said the waitress and walked off with the empties.

Les watched her for a moment then turned to Bodene. 'Okay Menny,' he said, dramatising a little. 'We're both busy men. Let's get down to cases. Warren tells me you had a film script knocked off, and you think I might be able to find it.'

'Maybe yes. Maybe no. Maybe I dunno, you know. But you were very good before,' said Bodene.

'And you were very generous,' said Les. He nodded towards the Rex Hotel. 'Not far from here, either.'

'Not far at all,' nodded Bodene.

'So where did this happen?' asked Les.

'Outside my pizza shop,' said Bodene. 'It was in bag in the back of my Mercedes.'

'Right,' nodded Les. Just then two cars started bipping each other and another concrete mixer rumbled up spewing diesel fumes everywhere. At the same time a little white dog under a table started yapping at a bigger one passing by. 'Shit! It's noisy here,' said Les. 'It's a wonder you don't have a coffee at your place, where it's a bit quieter.'

Menny gestured. 'I have to get out. Otherwise is like I'm married to the job.'

'Fair enough, I suppose,' agreed Les. 'But I didn't know you were into the film game, Menny.'

'Hey,' said Bodene, 'this is Bondi-Wood on the sea. What else do you do round here?'

'That's true,' nodded Les.

'Actually, I'm making two movies,' smiled Bodene.

'Two?'

'Yes.' An ironic smile flickered around Bodene's eyes. 'You know what I like about Australia, Les?'

'What?' said Les.

'You're weak.'

'Weak? Hey, turn it up, Menny. Haven't you heard of the Anzac spirit? Our bronzed Aussie life-savers?'

'I don't mean like that,' gestured Bodene. 'You're weak because you want to appease everybody. You roll over and let the world scratch your stomach and kick your arse at the same time. Political correctness. And to make bad with the worst: conspicuous compassion.'

'Conspicuous compassion?' queried Les.

'Yessss,' sniggered Bodene. 'Look at me everybodys. I'm crying for what happened to the stolen generation. Look at me everybodys. I've got my mouth taped up for the peoples in the detention centre. Look at me everybodys. I'm rolling in dog shits for the childrens overboard.' Bodene gestured dismissively. 'Is bullshit.'

Les thought for a moment. 'You know, you're half right, Menny.'

'Of course I'm right,' smiled Bodene. 'And if you say different, Les, I call you a racist.'

'Hey. As you should, mate. You're a wog.'

'In my country,' asserted Bodene, 'these bullshit peoples don't last five minutes before they get knife in ribs. Charity begins at home in Albania. Is that right, Lasjoz?'

'Is right for sure bastard,' growled the big man.

'I see what you mean,' agreed Les. 'If these ... conspicuous compassionistas carried on about the old diggers and kids with cancer as much as they do about illegal immigrants and such, we might be a lot better off.'

'Yes. But there's no show and glow for them in that, Les,' said Barbara.

'Exactly,' agreed Bodene. 'So what I'm going to do to get started, Les, is make most politically correct, conspicuously compassionate movie ever filmed.'

'You are?' queried Les.

'Hundred per cent,' enthused Bodene. 'Director and producer will be critically acclaimed. It will scoops the pool at Australian Film Industry Awards. All the actors will get warm inner glow, hot enough to melt Antarctica. Film Council will finance me to buggery. And,' beamed Bodene, 'best part is, no one in right mind will go see this load of critically acclaimed horse shits. So me, being wog producer, I can put more horse shits on Australian general public for being insensitive racist bastards, and take moral high ground, enough to give me nosebleed. I can't go wrong. They might even make stamp and name street after me.'

Les drew back. 'I'm in the presence of genius.'

'Tell me about it, Dude.' Menny took an envelope from a bag at his feet and handed it to Les. 'Here. Read this. Is . . .' He turned to the girls. 'What is word? I can never say.'

'Synopsis,' replied Topaz.

'That is the one. Sirnopsusis. Anyway. Movie is called *Gone With the Willy Willy*. Read on, my friend Les. You like. Writer does good job.'

Les carefully opened the envelope then took out a sheet of neatly typed foolscap paper and started reading.

GONE WITH THE WILLY WILLY
POST NO GRAVY PRODUCTIONS AUSTRALIA

This is the sensitive and ambitiously moving story of Dulcie Dugong, a hygenically challenged, hunchbacked, Aboriginal lesbian from Alice Springs. Dulcie, after drinking a flagon of '72 Grange Hermitage, confronts her demons and hitchhikes to Woomera. There she breaks into Baxter Detention Centre and frees Ibrahim, a gay, HIV positive, Lebanese Muslim asylum seeker. Pursued by crypto-fascist police and a gang of neo-Nazi skinhead kangaroo shooters, Dulcie and Ibrahim happen upon an outback Ku Klux Klan rally, where they steal the Grand Dragon's Holden Kingswood and flee to Sydney. There they meet up with Mehitebel, a friend of Dulcie's from when they were temporary visitants of the correctional system. Mehitebel, a diabetic single mother with a glass eye and a club foot, works at the heroin injecting centre in Kings Cross and lives in a housing commission home at Redfern with her thalidomide son, Sherwin, an asthmatic with a blocked heart valve. Dulcie receives an Arts Council grant to write a book of gay and lesbian poetry and uses some of the money to buy Sherwin a solar-powered wheelchair. The group join a non-gender-specific forest alliance, become vegans, and although economically marginalised, find commonality of purpose and co-exist happily until their harmonious existence is suddenly threatened by Mehitebel's next-door neighbour, Hurlbert, a sexist, homophobic warder at Long Bay Gaol with a primitive masculine identity problem. Hurlbert is also a member of the Sporting Shooters' Association, owns two Rottweilers he feeds baby seal meat and is an organiser for One Nation. Despite their tribulations and Dulcie's contradictions, Dulcie, Ibrahim and Mehitebel forge a lasting relationship on a tri-level basis of understanding and go on a journey of discovery. On their journey, they find spirituality, sexuality and social justice culminating in Ibrahim editing a gay newspaper and becoming the first Muslim to have a float in the Gay Mardi Gras. To add to their joy, Sherwin takes bronze in the men's backstroke at a handicapped swimming carnival and Hurlbert dies after accidentally shooting himself in the head while cleaning one of his guns.

Les glanced through the synopsis again, then carefully folded it back in its envelope and returned everything to Bodene.

'Well, what do you think, Les?' asked Bodene. 'Pretty good, huh!'

'What do I think?' replied Les. 'Menny. It . . . it's brilliant.'

'You like?'

'I do. Yes,' nodded Les. 'Except for one small thing.'

'Oh? What's that?' questioned Bodene.

'There's no Jews in there. You've left out the Jews.'

'Jews?'

'Yeah. They're a minority group,' explained Les. 'And a very important one, too. Leave them out, and people will say you're anti-Semitic.'

'Anti-Semitic?' Bodene looked shocked. 'Hey. Don't tell me about anti-Semitic and Jews. During the war, my grandfather Zoltan and my uncles Laszlo and Gyorgy were in the White Eagle Brigade. They killed hundreds of Jews. I know plenty about Jews, boy.'

Les shook his head. 'That's . . . very good, Menny,' he said. 'But it won't help your movie. You've got to have a Jew in it. And he's got to be a Holocaust survivor too.'

'Shit!' Bodene quickly opened the envelope and hurriedly read through the synopsis. 'Shit! You're right,' he said. Menny paused and thought for a moment. 'Okay. I know what I'll do. I'll make Dulcie's neighbour on the other side a Jew. Schlomo. And I'll also make him a dwarf.'

'A dwarf, Jewish, Holocaust survivor. That's fantastic, Menny,' said Les. 'You've hit the politically correct jackpot there.'

Bodene suddenly got excited. 'And ... and ... What about this, Les? When Sherwin wins the medal at the swimming, Schlomo throws a big party. And on the wall he hangs a huge photo of Adolf Hitler.'

'Adolf Hitler?' said Les.

'Yes. And the peoples say to him, "Schlomo, after all you went through, you put a photo of Hitler on your wall. Why?" And Schlomo holds up his arm. Smiles. And shows them the numbers tattooed on his arm. "Hey. See these numbers," he says. "I put them in at newsagents, and win Powerball. Five million dollars. Now I spend the rest of my life. Heil Hitler."'

Les stared at Bodene, shaking his head in amazement. 'That's fantastic, Menny,' he said. 'Absolutely fantastic. But unfortunately, mate, political correctness isn't about being happy.'

'It's not?' queried Menny.

'No,' replied Les. 'It's all about grief and sorrow. And making people feel miserable and guilty about themselves. You can't have a happy ending to your movie, Menny. They'll laugh at you.'

Bodene thought for a moment. 'You're right,' he agreed. 'I forget. Conspicuous compassion.'

'Exactly. So what about this,' suggested Les. 'The party's in full swing, and who should walk in the door? A Maori suicide bomber protesting about the Treaty of Waitangi. He detonates his explosives belt and kills everybody. Then, as the dust settles on all the blood and guts, and the smoke drifts away in the wind,'

Les slowly moved his hand for emphasis, 'the words materialise on-screen: *Gone with the Willy Willy*. Roll credits. Light the lights.' Les smiled confidently. 'What do you reckon?'

Bodene stared at Les. 'What do I reckon?' he said, reaching across and shaking Norton's hand. 'Les. You are genius. You should be writing movies yourself.' Bodene turned to the others. 'What do you think?'

The others all nodded in agreement.

'Is good idea. I like very much,' said Lasjoz.

'Hey,' shrugged Les. 'Making an Australian movie ain't rocket salad.'

'Don't I know,' said Bodene.

'Only trouble is, Menny,' sighed Les. 'They've knocked off your script. So you're kind of stuffed.'

'No, no. Not at all,' gestured Bodene. '*Gone with the Willy Willy* is only movie to get me established as brilliant, critically acclaimed, Australian film producer. The movie I want to make money with, the one bastards stole my script for,' cursed Bodene, 'that I pay bloke in Melbourne plenty to write, is called *The Case of the Talking Pie Crust*.'

'The case of the what?' asked Les.

Bodene eased back and smiled at Norton. 'Les,' he said, 'have you ever heard of Emile Mercier?'

Les thought for a moment, then shook his head. 'No. I can't say I have.'

'Hah!' laughed Bodene. 'I know more about Australia than some of you so-called dinky-di Aussies.'

Just then, the waitress came back and placed their coffees on a sandstone block in front of them. After she put Norton's cappuccino down, he slipped her twenty dollars. Not too ostentatiously. But enough for Bodene and the others to notice. Specifically Bodene. 'Keep that for yourself,' Les said quietly into the girl's ear.

'Thank you very much, sir,' smiled the girl.

As she walked away, the Albanian gangster's smile vanished. 'Les. What you are doing?' he demanded. 'I pay for this.'

'I know that, Menny,' shrugged Les. 'I was just giving the girl a tip. That's all. She works hard.'

'Oh. Oh.' Bodene was impressed by Norton's generosity. So were the others.

Les dropped a packet of sugar in his cappuccino, stirred it and took a sip. 'Hey. This is bloody good coffee,' he said.

'Yes. Yes it is,' nodded Bodene. He sugared his coffee and took a sip. 'Now. Where was I?'

'Emile Mercier,' said Les.

'Yes. Right.' Bodene had another sip of coffee. 'Okay. Emile Mercier was Sydney cartoonist back in nineteen forties and fifties for old newspaper called *The Sun*. This was before your time and mine, Les my friend. But believe me, back then Sydney was super squaresville. Pubs close at six o'clock. No TV. No rock 'n roll. Wear bikini on beach, say word bloody, get you arrested.'

'I've seen photos,' said Les.

'Women look like frumps. Men dress like shitkickers,' continued Bodene. 'Unless you bookmaker or crooked cop or politician. No one got money. No better than Russia.'

'Price often mentions that,' agreed Les.

'Yet this man, Emile Mercier, draw fabulous cartoons. Funny as circus. Take piss from everything. Make everybody laugh fit to bust.'

'And how did you get onto him?' asked Les.

'Through students at pizza shop.'

'Students?'

'Yes. Students live in Bellevue Hill. Buy pizzas from me,' said Bodene. 'Two are French. Same as Emile Mercier's family. They study him at university and show me copies of cartoons he does. Plus comic book called *Super Dooper Man*. And *The Case of the Singing Pie Crust*.'

'*The Singing Pie Crust*?' said Les.

'Exactly,' Bodene nodded over his coffee. 'So I start thinking. Lot of movies today are digitilised cartoons. Like *Shrek*. *Happy Feet*. *Ice Age*. You know the ones, Les.'

'Sure. Warren brings home the videos,' said Les. 'They're good.'

'So I think again. Why not make Australian movie about dysfunctional Australian family? Make it half Emile Mercier cartoons and half actors. And call it *The Case of the Talking Pie Crust*. Australians like a good laugh at themselves. They'd lap it up.'

'Sounds good to me,' said Les. 'Sort of *Who Killed Roger Rabbit?* meets *The Castle*.'

'Right on,' nodded Bodene.

'Have you got the money to make the movie?' asked Les.

Bodene answered Norton's question with a dismissive wave. 'Money is no problem,' he said. 'Only problem is, pricks knock off my script. Plus floppy disc and three little books of Emile Mercier cartoons. Which also cost me plenty and are impossible to replace.'

'And this is what you're willing to pay fifty thousand to get back?' said Les.

'Fifty. Maybe more,' said Bodene.

Les stared at Bodene for a moment. 'Okay. I'll give it a lash.'

'Give it a lash,' smiled Bodene. 'You sound like person in Emile Mercier cartoon.'

'Whatever,' Les smiled back. 'All right. So when did all this stuff go missing again?'

'Thursday. Thursday afternoon.'

'And it was in a bag, in the back of your car?'

'That's right.'

'What sort of bag?' Les gestured. 'A post bag? An overnight bag?'

Bodene exchanged glances with Barbara and looked uneasy. 'Actually. It was an old woman's handbag,' he admitted.

'An old woman's handbag?' said Les.

'A green one,' nodded Barbara. 'With a black eagle on the side.'

Bodene was about to speak, when his expression changed and he gave Lasjoz a nod. The big man rose out of his chair and stepped across to one of the gleaming Harley Davidsons. He put a helmet on that was hanging off the handlebars, then got on board and started the engine, revving it loud enough to shake the life out of the other punters seated outside Azulejos and almost blow the froth off Norton's cappuccino. Les watched as Lasjoz jumped the Harley over the gutter, then circled the roundabout several times, revving the engine every time he changed gears. The noise was horrendous and set the alarms off in several cars parked nearby. Finally, he drove the big American bike back to its original position, parked it and switched off the engine. After the racket from the Harley, any noise the council workers were making sounded like children playing. Les watched Lasjoz squeeze himself back into his chair then turned to Bodene.

'What was all that about?' asked Les.

'Battery in motorbike is flat,' replied Bodene. 'Have to give it charge now and again.'

'Fair enough.' Les had a sip of coffee then looked up at Bodene. 'Now what's all this about a bag with an eagle on the side?'

'Is nothing really,' said Bodene. 'Thursday morning I was looking at house in Rose Bay. Deceased estate. Some of the old woman's things were still in house and in closet, amongst all the shit, I notice green bag with black eagle on side, looks like eagle on Albanian flag. So I say, hey yes. I have this. I give to Barbara. Estate agent doesn't notice. So I throw it in back of car where I have film script. And ... I don't know, maybe for good luck, I put film script and everything in green bag.' Bodene rolled his eyes. 'Some fucking luck. Bag and everything else gets stolen. Bastards.'

'Yeah. You can say that again,' agreed Les. He drained his coffee and smiled at Bodene. 'So all up, I'm looking for a green handbag with a black eagle on the side, containing a script, a floppy disc and three books of cartoons by a bloke called Emile Mercier.'

Bodene was about to speak when two tall, dark-featured men appeared alongside him. They had impassive Slavic faces and sported plenty of bling with their smart casual clothes. Bodene stood up and greeted the men with equal impassivity, Lasjoz came to life and they all started talking in Albanian.

Les smiled at the two girls, gave the men a few polite moments then figured it might be time to leave. He caught Bodene's eye. 'Well, thanks for the coffee, Menny,' he said. 'I might get going. I think I've got everything I need to know. So I'll be in touch. Where's the best place to find you?'

'Down here, Les,' replied Bodene. 'Is good coffee. And gives me break from shop.'

'Fair enough. And I've got your phone number. I'd better give you mine.' Les took a Biro and a piece of paper from the side pocket of his cargoes, scribbled his phone number down and handed it to Bodene. 'There you go, Menny. If you need me, give me a call.'

Bodene shook Norton's hand. 'Thank you, Les,' he said sincerely. 'Let's hope you can do something.'

'It's only been the once,' winked Les, 'but I haven't let you down yet.'

'No. You are good man. You have not.'

'Goodbye, Barbara. Topaz.'

'Bye, Les,' smiled Topaz.

'Nice to meet you too Lasjoz.'

'Same for you, Les,' growled the big man.

Norton turned and walked away just as the waitress in the BUCKWHEAT T-shirt came out of the café carrying two coffees. At the same time, a jackhammer started up amidst the roadworks and another concrete mixer rumbled up amongst the dust and exhaust fumes with its air brakes hissing, while two motorists started beeping their horns and abusing each other. To add to the din, the little dog under the table started yapping at another dog again. Les caught the waitress's eye and pointed to his ears.

'Christ. How do you put up with all this bloody noise?' he asked her.

'It's been like it for weeks,' she shrugged. 'I'm used to it.'

Les shook his head. 'You're a better woman than I am, Gunga Din,' he replied, before crossing to the opposite side of the road. Mulling over his meeting with Bodene Menjou, Les strolled past the panel-beating shop and the Rex Hotel TAB, then idly glanced through the wide doorway leading into the lounge at several people seated amongst the tables. Sitting at bench table just back from the old surfboat hanging from the ceiling was his old fishing mate, Gary Jackson, and two other blokes Les had met before, but whose names he couldn't remember. They were all dressed in shorts and T-shirts and Gary had his denim cap squashed onto his head as usual. On the table in front of them were three half-empty schooners and an untidy mess of racing forms. Les slowed his step, thought for moment, then turned around and walked into the lounge bar. Gary noticed him approaching and looked up smiling.

'Les, mate,' he beamed. 'How are you, me old currant bun?'

'Good thanks, Jacko,' replied Les. 'How's yourself?'

'I'm all right.' Gary indicated his two friends. 'You know the boys.'

'Yeah,' nodded Les. 'How are you fellahs?'

'Good, Les,' replied the one with short blond hair.

'Les,' nodded his dark-haired mate, sporting what was probably the last mullet in the Eastern Suburbs.

'So what's doing, Les?' asked Gary.

'Gary,' enquired Les, 'those two mates of yours, Short Round and Weasel. Are they still taking things from people that don't belong to them?'

'Yes,' replied Gary. 'What are you after? They got some good sheepskin seat covers at the moment.'

'No. I'm not after any seat covers,' said Les. 'I'm after a green woman's handbag with a black eagle on the side.' Les made an open handed gesture. 'Now, God forbid, I'm not necessarily saying one of them took it. But it belongs to a mate of mine's grandmother. And it's got some papers and things in it she needs. So,' continued Les, 'it's just possible they, or one of your vast network of friends, might know something. Yeah?'

Gary nodded slowly. 'I'll ask them when I see them. And I'll, ah ... put the word out as well.'

'Thanks, Gary,' said Les. 'I'll give you my mobile phone number.' Les reached down for his Biro. 'And if you do happen to find out anything, Gary, there'll be a particularly nice drink in it for you.'

Gary rubbed his hands together gleefully and closed his eyes. 'We can always do with a drink, Les,' he said.

While Les was writing the number down on a coaster, Gary's mate with the mullet looked up from his form guide.

'Hey Les,' he said carefully. 'I notice Price has got one racing in the third at Rosehill today. Barrow Boy. Do you know anything?'

Les handed Gary the coaster and tightened his face. 'I'm not supposed to say anything. But yeah. It's a good thing. I've just been to the TAB myself. That's why I'm down here.'

'Shit!' Mullet circled the horse in his form guide.

'It says eight to one here,' said Gary's friend with the blond hair.

'Yeah. I got a bit better than that at the TAB.' Les put his Biro back in his cargoes and turned to leave. 'Anyway. I got to get going. And hey. I never told you anything. Okay?'

Mullet motioned as if he was zipping his mouth. 'No. Sweet, Les. I haven't seen you. None of us have.'

'You weren't here,' said his blond mate.

'Good,' nodded Les. 'Okay, Gary. I might hear from you.'

'No worries, Les,' replied Gary.

Ahh, you can't help but like Jacko and his mates, smiled Les, as he continued on up Glenayr Avenue. Staunchies to the last. I just hope they don't lose too much money on that old hayburner of Price's. Shit! The last I heard, Barrow Boy was in worse shape than that woman in Bodene's silly bloody movie and on its way to the glue factory. Les headed home, stopping once in Hall Street to get the papers.

Back at Chez Norton Les made himself comfortable in the loungeroom with a big Fuji apple and started perusing the papers. He was reading a column in the *Australian* when the phone rang.

'Hello?'

'Hello, you lazy big prick. What are you doing?'

'Getting bigger and lazier by the minute. How are you, Billy?'

'All right. Lyndy tells me you rang earlier. You're still crook.'

'Yeah. I'm heaps better than I was. But I thought, bugger it. I'll take a few more days off. Royce is going all right, isn't he?'

'Yeah. Good as gold,' said Billy. 'Some sheila even gave him her phone number last night.'

'Yeah? Well he's not a bad-looking bloke. So, been any dramas up there?' asked Les.

'Not really,' said Billy. 'Anything been happening with you?'

'Sort of,' replied Les.

Les told Billy about his meeting with Bodene and the others. What Menny was offering to get his script back and how he intended to become a critically acclaimed Australian film producer. Billy had a good laugh then settled down.

'I've seen that Lasjoz bloke around,' said Billy. 'He's a monster. But there's something a bit strange about him.'

'How do you mean?' asked Les.

'I dunno. Just something. But I'll tell you what, Les,' advised Billy. 'Be careful with Menny. I know we put a bit of shit on him now and again, but he can be a bad cunt if you cross him.'

'I'm well aware of that, Billy,' said Les. 'But I'm only looking for a film script. Which I doubt very much is going to turn up anyway.'

Billy went quiet on the phone for a moment. 'Hey, I got to go, Les. I got to take the boys to soccer.'

'Righto, Billy. I'll give you a yell through the week.'

'See you then, mate.'

Les replaced the phone and sat back for a few seconds. Something strange about Lasjoz, eh. Yeah. His bloody head. It's a big as a dump bin. But it can't be too bad if he's got a girlfriend like Topaz. Les dropped his apple core in the kitchen tidy and went back to reading the papers.

By the time he got to the weekend magazines Les was getting restless. He didn't particularly feel like going down the beach and having a run. He didn't feel like a paddle on his ski, either. In the backyard he'd rigged up a scaffold and a heavy bag. That would do splendidly. Les changed into a pair of old shorts, a black T-shirt and a sweatband cut from another black T-shirt, then after a glass of water, put the ghetto blaster on again, donned a pair of mitts and pounded the bag mercilessly for half an hour. This was followed with a series of crunches and throwing a kettlebell around for fifteen minutes. By then Les was in a lather of sweaty BO and badly in need of a shower. After getting cleaned up, Norton's stomach was rumbling and he was badly in need of more food. He drained a bottle of mineral water, changed back into what he was wearing before and walked down to the Hakoah Club.

Being Saturday, it was quieter than normal. But there were still plenty of people in there eating, drinking or pumping their hard-earned through the poker machines. Les had a steak and vegetables, followed by mudcake and ice cream. After that Les was in dire need of a coffee. The coffee at Hakoah was *very* good and Les had coffeed at almost every scene in Bondi. But he felt like a latte at his favourite coffee shop. His scene.

Directly across from the Hakoah Club was a café called Gabrielle's and Liza's that also doubled as a secondhand bookshop. The open dining area was at the front, then you stepped up into three large rooms with polished wooden floors and walls crammed with shelves of great books: everything from Jack Kerouac to Vladimir Nabokov; Aldous Huxley to the Rubaiyat of Omar Khayyam. The rooms contained large wooden tables and comfortable chairs, where students or whoever liked to sit with their notebooks and laptops studying or doing research. Les preferred the first room, where he liked to sit on a comfortable old blue Chesterfield set against the wall. The stocky, brown-haired woman that ran the place knew Les by sight and always gave him a smile when he entered, as did the staff in the kitchen. There was always a good sort in there to catch your eye and some of the staff at the Kelly Club who lived in Bondi had claimed Gabrielle's and Liza's as their scene also. Les liked nothing better than to bump into his workmates and catch up on a bit of gossip around town over a blueberry bagel and coffee that was, in Norton's opinion, the best in Bondi.

When Les walked in the owner gave him her customary warm smile and Les was pleased to find dark-haired Jimmy the barman from work sitting in the first room with two of the waitresses: copper-haired Louise, a country girl from Blayney, and Jenny, a rope-haired blonde who grew up in Five Dock. They were all casually dressed in T-shirts and jeans and just as happy to see Les as he was to see them. Les ordered a latte and pulled up a chair.

Three lattes for Les and a lot of laughs later they all went their separate ways and Les found himself at home again, fired up with caffeine, wondering what to do with himself. He was in the kitchen glugging down water and hoping to dissolve some of the toxins when his mobile phone rang on the table. Les picked it up and pushed the green button.

'Hello?'

'Hello Les, my main man. My rock. How are you, mate?'

'Price,' smiled Les. 'Don't tell me. Let me guess. You're at the races.'

'And killing them,' chortled Price.

'Hello. What have you done this time, you villain?'

'What have I done?' answered Price. 'Well, for starters, I've taken that fat turd Harold Hedges to the cleaners for over three hundred grand. You should see the shit of a thing. His face looks like a dropped pie.'

'How ... what?' asked Les.

'Barrow Boy,' wheezed Price. 'He waltzed home by two lengths. And, at the sweet odds, I might add, of nine to one.'

Norton's jaw dropped. 'You're kidding?'

'No. I've been planning this for months,' chortled Price. 'I've cleaned them all out. I've tugged over a mill. I'll need a wheelbarrow to collect the money. Two wheelbarrows.' Price suddenly started singing into the phone. 'Barrow Boy, Barrow Boy. All you had to do was back . . . old Barrow Boy.'

Les could picture Price dancing round the Members' Lounge with a Scotch in one hand and his mobile in the other. 'Jesus, you're not bad, Price. I've got to give it to you.'

'Yes. I have my moments,' rejoined Price. 'And I'm sorry I couldn't let on. But I had to play this one extremely close to my chest.'

'That's okay. I'm not as keen as I was on the punt anyway.'

'But I promise. When you get back to work. Boh–nusss.'

'Thanks, Price,' said Les. 'That's very nice of you.'

'And talking about work,' said Price, 'when are you coming back? Billy said you're still a bit crook.'

'Yeah. I'm not a hundred per cent, Price. But I reckon I should be okay by the end of next week, with a bit of luck.'

'Yeah. Well, don't leave it too long. I breathe easier when my ace man's out the front.'

'Don't worry, Price,' Les assured him. 'I'll be there.'

'Good. Shit! I've got to go. They just jumped at Flemington. Give me a ring through the week.'

'Okay, boss. See you then.'

Les clicked off, put his mobile back on the kitchen table and shook his head. Bloody Barrow Boy. That cunning, shifty old bastard. He's unreal. One thing for sure, grinned Les. Gary and his mates down the pub will think the sun shines out of my arse. Anyway. What now? Les walked into the loungeroom and picked up the TV guide to find Easts were playing Balmain on Foxtel. He tuned in as the Tigers converted a try to lead 8–2. Les settled back on the lounge and was absorbed in the game when the front door opened and Warren clomped down the hallway and stepped into the loungeroom, wearing cowboy boots, a pair of jeans and a red and white striped shirt, and looking tired and in need of a shave.

Les greeted him brightly. 'Woz. How are you, mate?'

'Just,' Warren replied glumly.

'Funny you should say that,' enthused Les. 'I've never seen you looking better.'

'Yeah.' Warren went to the bathroom and came back with four Panadeine capsules. He got a glass from the kitchen, made himself a Jack Daniel's and Coke and washed them down with half his drink.

'Feel all right now?' Les asked him.

'Yeah,' replied Warren, his eyes spinning as he downed another good mouthful of bourbon. 'Yeah. I do.'

'Good. So where's Ugly Betty?'

'Home getting packed. You don't think I'd bring her round here, do you? You were always trying to grass-cut me with Clover. It'd be the same with Beatrice.'

'Yeah. You're right, Woz,' said Les. 'It's all I can do to stop myself from tearing all the buxom wench's clothes off, and ravishing her in front of you.'

Warren sat down on a lounge chair and half looked at the TV. 'So did you meet up with Bodene Menjou?'

'Yes. I did actually,' replied Les.

Les told Warren about his meeting with Menny. Including the two film scripts, the noise at Azulejos, Topaz and Bodene's big friend. Warren listened intently, getting up once to make himself another Jack Daniel's and Coke.

'So bottom line,' said Warren, eased back in his lounge chair. 'You're looking for a green handbag with a black eagle on the side.'

'That's about it, Woz,' said Les.

'You sound like Sam Spade and *The Case of the Maltese Falcon*.'

'Whatever,' shrugged Les. 'But if I fluke it, fifty grand could fall in. Maybe even more, yet already.'

Warren stared at Les for a moment then glanced at his watch. 'Anyway. I'd better make a move.'

'You sure you don't want a lift out to the airport?' asked Les.

Warren shook his head. 'No. I'm good.'

'Okay.'

Les went back to his football. Warren took his empty glass out to the kitchen then went to his room and packed his bags. Easts were leading by two points when Warren walked back into the lounge and sat down. He was still wearing the same jeans, but he'd changed into a clean denim shirt.

'Shit I envy you, Woz,' said Les. 'You and the beautiful Beatrice, up there in that warm Queensland sunshine. Eating mud crabs. Drinking untold bottles of chilled Portaloo Sauvignon. You're a lucky bastard.'

'Yeah terrific,' muttered Warren. 'The film crew are a bunch of over-aged fuckin emos. And I've also got to deal with a team of whingeing, argumentative wog racing-car drivers who think their shit doesn't stink.'

'The correct expression, Warren,' chided Les, 'is Latin temperament.'

Warren was about to say something when a horn beeped outside. 'Shit! Here's my driver.' Warren stood up and straightened his jeans. 'Okay. I have to get going. I'll see you when I get back.'

'All right, Woz. You take care. And say hello to Ugly Betty for me.'

'I will.'

The front door opened and closed, leaving Les to his football, with Easts ending up winners by six points. A result even sweeter for Les because Balmain had three tries disallowed and George Brennan would be spewing. Les walked out to the kitchen to get another big juicy Fuji apple when his mobile phone rang.

'Hello?'

'Les. How are you, mate? It's Jacko.'

'Gary,' smiled Les. 'How's things?'

'How's things?' slurred Gary. 'Well, how do you think things are, mate? Barrow Boy. Ten to one on the TAB.'

'You backed it.'

'Backed it? Me'n Ray had the double. Arthur had the double and boxed the trifecta. Plus we backed it. We've cleaned up.'

'Good on you,' said Les sincerely, picking up on the noise in the background. 'So now I imagine you're having a quiet drink.'

'Quiet drink. Quiet fuckin drink. None of us are going home,' rasped Gary.

'Well, why not,' said Les.

'Hey, Jesus you're a good bloke, Les,' said Gary. 'Thanks for that.'

'My pleasure, mate. But remember, you never got it from me. Okay?'

'Les. Say no more. Say no more.'

'Exactly,' replied Les.

'Anyway,' said Gary. 'I've rung up to return the favour.'

'You have?'

'Bloody oath I have!' declared Gary. 'You know Irish John. The Postman.'

'Irish John? Yeah,' nodded Les. 'He's not a bad bloke. But he's a shocking pisspot.'

'Yeah. Well, we all know that. Anyhow. His run goes up near the fire station on the corner of Old South Head and ...'

'Gilgandra,' said Les. 'I know a girl lives up there.'

'Right,' answered Gary. 'Well, down the end of Brassie Street, Irish John said there's a team of shifties living in a house, don't do much work.'

'Go on.'

'Anyway. Irish John reckons he's doing the mail up there. And he saw one of them walk into the house carrying a green bag with a black eagle on the side.'

Norton's ears pricked up. 'Irish John told you this?'

'As sure as I'm standing here, Les.'

'Righto. Give me the address.' Les got a Biro and wrote it down. 'And Irish John's fair dinkum about this?'

'Mate. He's over playing pool,' said Gary. 'You want me to go and get him?'

'No. Don't bother,' said Les. 'All right, Gary, thanks for that. I'll go round and have a look.'

'No worries. And thanks again for the other, Les.'

'Any time, mate.'

Les hung up then sat down in the kitchen and took a chomp on his apple. He had another look at the address, then got the street directory from the phone cabinet and came back to the kitchen. Brassie ran between Gilgandra and Warners; about five minutes' drive away. Les closed the street directory and looked out the kitchen window. Noticing it was getting dark, he glanced at his watch. I'll have a bite to eat and watch TV for a while, he thought, then go round and see what's going on. But between Jacko and Irish John half full of ink, you can bet I'll be wasting my time. Les finished his apple then made himself a Promite sandwich with all the trimmings and took it into the loungeroom with a cup of tea.

The TV was off, it was completely dark outside and Les was standing in the kitchen dressed in a black bomber jacket, the same grey T-shirt, Levis and a pair of black, ten-hole Doc Martens. So what am I going to say to these kind folks when I knock on their door, he mused, absently jiggling his car keys. Good evening. My name's Les. Do you mind if I have the green bag with the eagle on the side, please? I know what they'll say. Les shook his head and stared out at the darkness. Oh well. Nothing ventured, nothing gained, I suppose. He switched off the lights and locked the house, then climbed behind the wheel of his battered Berlina and drove off.

The lounge at the Rex was in full swing as Les cruised past. But they were long gone at Azulejos when he turned left into Warners Avenue, and Barraclough Park was deserted when he hung a right into Brassie. The house was sitting between two other cottages facing a block of four home units near the end of the street. Les pulled up beneath a streetlight on the opposite side of the road and left the engine running while he checked it out.

It was an old, single-storey brick cottage with a white brick fence at the front divided by a metal gate. A short path lead through weeds and long grass to a small verandah and a front door set between two heavily curtained windows facing the street. A faint light shone through a small pane of stained glass on top of the door, and on the right an empty carport sat in front of a wooden gate leading to a passage running alongside the house. The house was in silence, the surrounding buildings were quiet and the street was empty. Les did a U-turn and parked down from the house with the car facing Warners Avenue, then got out and walked back.

The gate creaked slightly in the darkness when Les opened it; he closed it quietly behind him, then he stepped up and knocked on the door. There was no immediate answer. But Les was sure he heard movement inside. So he waited a few moments and knocked again. Footsteps sounded in the hallway, then the door opened and Norton found himself facing a lean man with a dark buzz cut and skinny sidelevers, wearing jeans and a dirty white T-shirt several sizes too big for him. From deep in a gaunt, lined face, two bloodshot eyes were spinning around like crazy and he oozed paranoia. Les snatched a quick glance behind the man and saw a short, badly lit hallway with two doors on either side and a dirty wooden floor that led to another door at the end. The man glared wild-eyed at Les, his face a volatile mixture of hatred and suspicion.

'Who the fuck are you?' he snarled. 'What do you fuckin want?'

'Mate,' said Les easily. 'All I want is a green bag. That's all.'

Les was about to explain it belonged to a friend of his, just give it back, he'd be on his way and there'd be no hard feelings, and if he was wrong he'd apologise, when suddenly the bloke started to hyperventilate and the crazed look on his face switched to complete lunacy.

'Green bag,' he shrieked. 'Green fuckin bag. I'll give you nothing, you cunt. I'll fuckin kill you.' Without warning, the man attacked Les in a hissing, cursing hail of punches and kicks.

Taken completely by surprise, Les hardly had time to defend himself and a couple of punches managed to get through, catching him on the eye and mouth, and a kick got him in the groin where luckily the fork in his jeans blunted the blow. However, the man was in such a heightened state of rage, his kicks and punches were mostly ineffective. Not wasting any time,

Les set himself and drilled the enraged man with a sizzling straight left, splitting both his lips. The bloke cursed, spat some blood, then came back swinging. Les nailed him with another, even harder, straight left followed by a filthy left hook that mashed the bloke's nose across his face and sent him reeling back down the hallway into the wall. Les tore after him and kicked him in the stomach and kneecap, kneed him in the balls then whacked him with another left hook and kicked him in the stomach again.

'You cunt,' the bloke howled. 'I'll fuckin kill you. I'll kill you.' The bloke gave a roar, then bounced off the wall, furiously throwing punches at Les.

Les moved to the side, set himself and belted the bloke with an awesome short right that shattered his jaw and knocked out several teeth. The bloke came straight back at Les, screaming obscenities and throwing punches. Blocking the punches, Les bashed the bloke with a left and a right, then took him by his bloodied T-shirt and slammed his head into the wall, before spinning him across the hallway and slamming his head into the opposite wall, then kicking out his other knee.

'You cunt,' screamed the man, still throwing punches through the pain and blood. 'I'll kill you, you cunt. I'll fuckin kill you.'

Les brought his boot up into the bloke's balls again, elbowed him twice across his broken jaw, then followed up with two more left hooks and another pulverising straight right that sent globs of blood spattering across the walls and floor.

'Ohh, you cunt. I'll kill you. I'll fuckin kill you.' Despite being on the end of a ferocious beating, the enraged man kept coming at Les, his lacerated face twisted into a mask of tortured anger.

Les ducked under another flurry of punches, grabbed the bloke round the knees then picked him up and body-slammed him hard onto the wooden floor, amost breaking his back.

'Aaarrgh! You cunt,' hollered the bloke, throwing punches from the floor. 'I'll kill you. I'll fuckin kill you.'

By now, Norton's blood was up. Feeling the bones crunching through his Doc Martens, he kicked all the bloke's ribs in along one side, then kicked him several times in the head. He jumped on him, jumped on him again, kicked all his other ribs in, kicked him in the kidneys then stomped on his head, grinding the bloke's face into the floor.

'Ohhhh, you cunt,' came a pitiful wail. 'I'll kill you. Fuckin kill you.' Slipping and sliding in his own blood, the bloke made an agonised attempt to get to his knees. 'You cunt,' he panted. 'You'll get nothing. I'll kill you. I'll fuckin kill you.'

'Jesus Christ!' railed Norton. 'What are you? A fuckin replicant?'

'Fuck you,' the bloke cursed.

'Yeah, and fuck you too.' Les stepped back and gave the bloke a solid kick in the ribs followed by another in the head that dropped him flat on his face.

'Aaarrghh, you cunt. I'll kill you. I swear to God. I'll fuckin kill you.'

Les was about to break one of the bloke's arms, when the front of the house was washed with light and a car pulled up in the driveway. Doors slammed and two men appeared in the doorway dressed much like Les. One had a mop of tight brown curls, the other's hair was dyed white and cut close to his scalp. The curly-haired man looked at Les, then noticed the bloke he'd been fighting lying on the floor covered in blood, still cursing Les and punching the air.

'Shit. That's Micah,' yelled the bloke with the curly hair. 'Get the cunt, Zack.'

'You go for his throat, Brett,' his mate yelled back, slamming the door shut behind him.

The two men charged straight at Les, who stepped back to ride the shock. At the same time, Micah managed to push himself to his knees and the two men tripped over his broken, battered body, tumbling clumsily into Les instead of tackling him. Behind a flailing tangle of arms and legs, Les was pushed backwards through the partially open door at the end of the hallway into a dimly lit room, knocking over a Laminex table behind him and everything on it. Managing to stay on his feet in the melee, Les had a moment or two to set himself before Brett scrambled up first, ready for another go.

Stepping back a little, Les pivoted and Brett walked straight into a right cross that sent him crashing over the nearest table, scattering the contents noisily across the room. Turning quickly to his left, Les just had time to move back as Zack swung a right front kick at his head. Norton stepped around the kick and caught Zack behind the knee with the crook of his right arm, smashed him in the face with a left backfist then slammed his left knee into Zack's back. Zack howled with pain, then howled again as Les swept him off his feet and he came down hard on his spine onto a heavy iron pot lying on the floor. Not wasting any time, Les stomped a Doc Martens into Zack's balls, then booted him in the solar plexus before kicking him in the temple, knocking him out cold.

Brett was still groggy. But he got to his feet and came at Les throwing wild punches from all angles. Les went underneath and doubled him up with four solid combination punches that made him gasp with pain. Almost in one movement, Les grabbed Brett by his mop of curly hair, held his head down and smashed his knee up into Brett's face, spreading his nose across his cheekbones. Still holding Brett's hair, Les let him fall towards the floor then spun his face around and pounded it with short rights till Brett's eyes rolled back and he went still. Hearing noises coming from the hallway, Les dropped Brett and stared apprehensively through the open door.

Micah was crawling aimlessly around the floor in circles, covered in blood and still cursing Les. 'Get out of here, you cunt,' he rasped. 'I'll fuckin kill you. I'll kill you.'

Noticing the heavy iron pot lying on the floor, Les picked it up and flung it at Micah's head, splitting it open. 'Ohh, shut the fuck up.'

'Ahhhrghhh. You rotten, fuckin cunt,' Micah howled painfully as the iron pot bounced off his bloodied head and clattered across the hallway. 'I'll kill you. I'll dead set fuckin kill you. You cunt.'

'Good.' Les ignored him and gazed around the faintly lit room. Besides those that had been knocked over, Les could make out another three tables stacked with gas rings, woks, pots, glass beakers, glass bowls, plastic trays, a set of scales, a pill press and other items, all being cooled by electric fans. The walls were covered with sheets of blue plastic and stacked against the walls were black drums with HAZCHEM markings on the sides; piled next to the drums were plastic bags of white powder and an assortment of other things. Fumes from a pot boiling on one of the tables caught in Norton's throat and eyes and Les didn't need a degree in chemistry to know he was standing in a drug lab. Stacked near a door in the corner were three brown plastic garden chairs and sitting on the top one was a green leather bag with an eagle on the side. Well, I'll be buggered, smiled Les. There's Bodene's bag. Unreal. I'll put it inside a plastic one to make sure nothing falls out, then hit the toe.

Les picked up an empty plastic bag from a pile on a table, and was about to walk across to the stacked chairs, when the door in the corner opened and a skinny, sallow-faced man with dark hair pulled back in a ponytail walked into the room. He was wearing a black T-shirt under a pair of khaki overalls, and cradled in a pair of heavily tattooed arms was a pump-action shotgun. The man spotted Les through the gloom and brought the barrel up.

For a brief moment Norton froze, then his adrenalin kicked in and he dropped the plastic bag and made a frantic leap to the right a split second before the bloke pulled the trigger and blasted a hole in the wall next to the hallway. The man swung the shotgun around and fired again, missing Les, but blowing a burner and the pot boiling on top of it across the room.

His eyes darting around the room, Les noticed a glass container half full of fuming liquid sitting on a table next to a whirling fan. Before Ponytail could pull the trigger again, Les snatched it up and threw the contents in Ponytail's face, making him scream, drop the shotgun and start tearing wildly at his eyes. Les flung the glass container aside, then picked the shotgun up by the barrel and swung the butt around, straight across Ponytail's face, smashing his fingers and all his front teeth. Ponytail fell back against the wall and Les clubbed him over the head with the shotgun, then kept clubbing him until Ponytail slumped to the floor, covered in blood.

Les lowered the shotgun and gave Ponytail a light kick in the ribs. He didn't move. Les gave him another, and again he didn't move. Les suddenly noticed the blood and hair all over the gun butt. Shit. I hope I haven't killed him, he thought. Ahh, fuck it. Too bad if I have. Les dumped the shotgun in the man's lap then picked up the plastic bag from where he'd dropped it and slipped the green bag inside, feeling the film script and the little books of cartoons as he did. He had a last look around then stepped into the hallway.

Micah was still crawling painfully around the bloodied floor muttering to himself. Les stepped around him and as he did, Micah made a desperate grab for Norton's leg and tried to bite him.

'I'll kill you, you cunt,' he spluttered through his torn and broken mouth. 'I'll fuckin kill you.'

'Ohh, why don't you get fucked.' Not feeling the best after almost getting blasted with a shotgun, Les stepped back and kicked Micah hard in the mouth, smashing several more teeth. 'Now shut the fuck up, you pain in the arse,' ordered Les, before kicking Micah in the face again.

'Ohhrrghhh. You gunt,' mumbled Micah, trying desperately to raise his battered and bleeding head. 'I'll gill you. I'll gill you. Grrhhggh. Ahgrrhh. Ohhhrrhh,' he garbled in frustration.

'Ohh, go fuck yourself.'

Les opened the front door and started to leave when he noticed a flicker of blue flame in the loungeroom. He meant to stop. But before Les knew it, he'd stepped outside onto the verandah and closed the door behind him. A worried look appeared on Norton's face. Shit. I hope the place isn't about to catch on fire. Noticing a silver Ford parked in the carport, Les walked over to have a look down the side passage when the sound of a dull explosion came from inside the house, and the room at the end of the hallway burst into flames. Les ran back to the front door when there was a louder explosion followed by another that blew the side windows out.

'Oh shit!' exclaimed Les. He was about to kick the door in when a ball of fire framed in the stained glass at the top, came roaring up the hallway. Les stepped back and shook his head. 'Sorry fellahs,' he said. 'You're on your own.'

Les walked smartly back to his car, opened the front door and threw the bag on the passenger seat just as a violent explosion racked the house, blowing away the guttering and sending a hail of roof tiles clattering onto the houses either side and into the street. Les got behind the wheel, started the car and drove off, not turning the lights on till he reached Warners Avenue. By the time he got there, a quick glance in the rear-vision mirror showed the house completely engulfed in bright red flames that lit up the street and sent showers of sparks spiralling into the night sky.

Les returned home via Old South Head Road and came down O'Brien Street past Menny's pizza shop. He hooked into Cox Avenue, then pulled up in front of Chez Norton, grabbed the plastic bag, locked the car and hurried inside.

'Holy fuckin shit!' exclaimed Les, switching on the lights and tossing the bag onto a chair in the loungeroom. 'And I said I couldn't get into too much trouble looking for a film script? I'm lucky I'm alive.' His eyes zeroed in on the liquor cabinet. 'Where's a bloody glass?'

Les poured himself a giant, enormous, Jack Daniel's and Coke then bolted down half in one go. His eyes spun and his cheeks reddened, then he hoofed down some more.

'Oh yeah,' exclaimed Les.

Les had another mouthful then left the rest on the kitchen table and went into the bathroom to check himself out. He had a fat lip, some bark missing and a mouse under his right eye. But that was about all. However, he was spattered with blood and there were globs of it stuck to his Doc Martens. Les stripped off completely and threw all his clothes in the washing machine, added a liberal dose of Dynamo plus a good splash of disinfectant, then switched the machine on the extra heavy cycle.

He finished his drink and, while his clothes were going round, hosed off his Doc Martens and left them out in the backyard to dry. After a long hot shower Les changed into a clean white T-shirt and a pair of loose-fitting grey shorts and, feeling better, poured himself another delicious then went into the loungeroom and sat down to inspect his find. I might have almost got killed, smiled Les, but I've survived. And now I'm fifty thousand in front. Maybe more if I string things out a little. Les winked towards the night sky. Thanks, boss. Les had a sip on his delicious, put it aside and removed the leather handbag from the plastic one.

'What?'

It wasn't an eagle on the side of the bag. It was a bat. And when Les opened the bag, instead of finding a film script, he found a black, bound ledger. What he thought were little books of cartoons turned out to be plastic bags full of little white pills. Les pushed the plastic on one bag up against the pills, and stamped on each pill was the outline of a bat. He opened the black bound ledger. Written down the first page was a list of initials and numbers, starting with JB — 200. BK — 500. JD — 500. MW — 1000. TN — 1000.

'Oh bugger it.'

Les dropped the ledger on the coffee table, stared at the green bag and its contents and cursed his luck. This is what they were cooking up in there. No wonder that ratbag attacked me when I mentioned green bag. He was wired up to the gills on speed and thought I was some heavy come round to rip off their dope. The bat's their brand name or whatever and the ledger's full of dealers and amounts. What a cock-up. Thanks to bloody Irish John, I stumbled onto a team of meth cooks and nearly got my head blown off over a bag of rotten fuckin Lou Reed. Les stared sourly at the green bag. Right. Well I know where all this is going.

Les took the bags of pills out of the green bag then carried them into the bathroom and tipped the lot down the toilet. It took more than one go. But before long, Les had flushed a fortune in speed through Bondi's sewerage system. After that, he got a pair of heavy duty scissors and cut the green bag up on the kitchen table along with the clear plastic ones, then compressed everything into a plastic shopping bag. Next, Les ripped all the pages out of the ledger with numbers and intials on them, tore them up and pushed them into the plastic shopping bag as well. Leaving the bag on the kitchen table, Les got a Wettex, some Spray and Wipe and a torch, then went outside and had a good look around the front of the car. There were a few smears of blood on the steering wheel and brake pedal, but that was all. Les cleaned everything off then stuffed the Wettex into the plastic bag with everything else. Satisfied, he went into his room and put on a pair of trainers for a quick stroll down to the coffee shop on the corner.

Leaving the house, Les knew he wasn't being over cautious. If someone took his number as he drove off and the police were able to connect him to four deaths in a drug lab, he'd be in very deep shit. And from a callous perspective, the unexpected fire was a good thing. It destroyed any evidence of him being there. As for Irish John and Jacko, if they did mention anything to him, he would simply say, yes, he drove round there. But the place had burnt down. What a bummer. Say no more. Say no more.

When he got to the coffee shop, Les opened their Otto bin and dropped the plastic bag inside, covering it with other rubbish. Convinced his arse was totally covered, Les brushed his hands and after a cursory look around, headed home to settle down in front of the TV with another delicious.

When he picked up the TV guide, Les rolled his eyes in disbelief. The Saturday night movie was *Speed*, with Keanu Reeves and Sandra Bullock. Yeah, that'd be right. Les couldn't be bothered checking out Foxtel. So he went to a pile of DVDs Warren had brought home from the advertising agency and chose *Walk the Line* with Joaquin Phoenix and Reese Witherspoon.

Les enjoyed it immensely and couldn't believe Joaquin Phoenix did all his own singing. He was great. So was Reese Witherspoon and the bloke who played Jerry Lee Lewis. Les also had to choke back a tear when Johnny Cash proposed to June Carter on stage and she said yes. By golly, sniffed Les, when the movie finished and he put the DVD away. You can't beat a feel-good movie. I might even buy the soundtrack.

By now Les was bone tired and drained. It's not every day you beat death by a whisker and have to fight a gang of nutters, after just getting over the flu. He switched off the lights, cleaned his teeth and climbed into bed. Tomorrow he would wake up happy and shiny to another delightful day in beautiful downtown Bondi; and make some more new friends. Les scrunched his head into the pillows, yawned once and nodded off.

Les woke up in reasonably good shape on Sunday morning to find it was cooler and cloudier than Saturday. He climbed out of bed, stretched out a couple of yawns, then went to the bathroom. There was no missing his fat lip and the mouse under his right eye. But compared to what could have happened, it was nothing. After finishing in the bathroom, Les went to the kitchen and put the jug on, then without bothering to get changed, climbed into his trainers and walked down to get the papers.

Back in the kitchen, Les made a pot of tea and decided what he'd have for breakfast. When everything was ready, he sat down relaxed and opened the *Telegraph*.

A nasty plane crash in Indonesia took up the first two pages. But on page three was a photo and the heading BONDI DRUG LAB EXPLODES IN FLAMES. FOUR BODIES FOUND. Les read avidly over his smoked salmon and scrambled eggs.

The story had come in late, and although the photo was dramatic and the journo had managed to beat the story up as best he could, it still didn't say any more than Les had surmised. A gun was found in the house. A burnt-out car was in the driveway. Police still hadn't identified the bodies. And despite

Bondi Fire Station being just round the corner, the blaze was so intense, firefighters couldn't save the house and were pleased they managed contain the fire to the immediate premises. Police said this was typical of the danger drug labs and other clandestine operations of this nature held for the public. Etc., etc., etc. One sentence made Norton laugh out loud over his scrambled eggs. Up until the explosions started, neighbours hadn't heard anything. Yeah, that'd be right, nodded Les. I almost kicked a screaming speed freak to death in the hallway. I fought two other blokes through a drug lab, knocking shit all over the place. A bloke fires a shotgun at me. Cars pull up. Doors are slammed. Blokes are yelling out at the tops of their voices. And the neighbours don't hear a thing. If someone had been in there smoking a joint and listening to Pink Floyd's *Dark Side of the Moon*, the cops would have been around before the fire alarm rings on track three. Les breezed through the rest of the paper then opened up the sports section.

'Oh shit,' chuckled Les. 'Have a look at this.'

Under the heading FLAMBOYANT CLUB OWNER PULLS OFF MASSIVE BETTING COUP was a photo of Price standing next to the jockey and trainer. He was holding onto Barrow Boy's bridle and grinning like a rat with a gold tooth.

'Good on you, mate,' said Les. 'Good on you.'

Les read the article and the football results, then got a pair of scissors and cut Price's article out for his scrapbook. After reading the comics to make sure Torkan had despatched the baddies and got the comely wench, Les opened the *Sun-Herald* to find the drug lab article and photo was almost identical to the *Telegraph*'s. Les finished the papers then put them aside and checked his watch. He poured another cup of tea and took it into the loungeroom to watch *Sunday*.

The fire at the drug lab was the third item on the news and apart from the old brick chimney, there was nothing left of the house. A tired-faced police commander reiterated the problem police faced with drug labs, then the news finished and it was onto the feature stories: the ice epidemic sweeping Sydney, and Melbourne gangsters.

The ice story centred mainly around some skinny gay bloke who'd lost count of how many blokes had bonked him while he was out skating over the last three years. But it was all cool. He was straight now and had his shit and his tush together. The Melbourne gangster story was better: a baby-faced killer who could still smile after getting a thirty-five-year lagging. But although he'd moved millions of dollars' worth of pills and either murdered or organised the murders of a raft of rivals in the drug trade, his parents said he was a terrific kid with a great sense of humour, loved animals and wouldn't hurt a fly. Well, that'd be right, agreed Les. If me and Eddie got arrested for all the people we've sent to an early grave, our parents would say the same about us. My oath they would. *Sunday* finished with a great story about a young Bondi girl who could play bass guitar like a demon and was killing them overseas.

Les cleaned up in the kitchen and by the time he'd put the last plate away, things were stirring inside him. Tea was always nice.

But the big red-headed Queenslander needed a cup of coffee. A flat white or a cappuccino would suffice. A crisp latte would be even better. Les changed into a clean pair of jeans, a blue Brazilian soccer T-shirt he bought at the op-shop in Hall Street and a black hooded tracksuit top. After plonking his baseball cap on his head, he put his mobile in the front pocket of his top, locked the house and strolled nonchalantly down to Gabrielle's and Liza's.

The owner and the staff gave him a welcoming smile when he walked in and Les was delighted to see Louise and Jenny, wearing jeans and fleecy tops waving to him from the old, blue Chesterfield inside. Les ordered a latte, eased his frame through the other punters and joined his two workmates.

'Hello, ladies,' smiled Les, pulling up a seat. 'How are you this morning?'

'Good, Les,' said Louise. 'How's yourself?'

'Not too bad, thanks,' replied Les.

'Shit! What happened to your face?' asked Jenny.

'I was sparring with a bloke down the surf club. And he got a bit carried away.'

'So I imagine you sorted him out,' said Jenny.

'Yes. You could say that,' replied Les.

'God. I'd hate to have your job,' said Louise.

'Yeah, well. Someone has to do it,' shrugged Les. He looked up as his coffee arrived, thanked the girl then turned to the others. 'So how was it up there last night?'

'How was it?' echoed Jenny exchanging glances with Louise. 'It was unreal.'

'Oh?' said Les, taking a sip of coffee.

'After work,' said Louise, 'we were having a few staffies. And Mr Galese came around with the biggest bag of money I've ever seen. And gave everyone a thousand dollars.'

'A thousand bucks?' said Les.

'Yes. Cash,' said Jenny. 'Fifties and hundreds.'

'Shit,' groaned Les. 'And I have to take the night off.'

'I've had my eye on this dress up in Bondi Junction for months,' said Louise. 'It'll be in my wardrobe tomorrow morning. With a matching handbag and shoes.'

'What a boss,' said Jenny, taking a sip of her flat white. 'Honestly. He's a saint.'

'He's a knight,' smiled Les. 'I can verify that.'

The girls were in a great mood as they all chit-chatted away over their coffees about work and other things. He also agreed with the girls that Billy's cousin Royce was a bit of a spunk and Eddie always looked sinister when he wore his black leather jacket. The conversation swung round to movies and Les was telling them about *Walk the Line* when his phone rang.

'Hello?'

'Is that Les Norton?'

'Yeah. Who's this?'

'You don't know me,' said the voice. 'But I'm a friend of Bodene Menjou's.'

'Hang on.' Les turned to the girls. 'I'll be back in a sec,' he said, then stood up and took his phone out onto the footpath. 'Now what did you just say? You're a friend of Bodene Menjou's.'

'That is right, my friend.' The voice was guttural and sounded foreign.

'So what are you ringing me for? And how did you get my phone number?'

'Through a mutual aquaintance.'

'All right,' said Les carefully.

'I hear you're looking for a film script. In a green bag with an eagle on the side.'

This took Les back a little. 'I could be,' he answered. 'What's it to you?'

'I might be able to help you,' said the voice.

'Oh? And what's your end?'

'Satisfaction. That's all.'

'Okay,' said Les, somewhat mystified.

A sudden sneeze sounded at the end of the line, before the voice asked. 'What are you doing today?'

'Not much. Having a coffee. Kicking back.'

'Go down to the Bondi Markets. Check out the stalls. And ask the woman who does the tarot reads. You might find what you're looking for.'

'The Bondi Markets?' said Les.

'That's right,' said the voice. 'I'll ring you back later.'

'Hang on. What …?' The voice hung up. Les thought for a

moment, then put his phone back in his top and went in to rejoin the others.

They ordered more coffees and talked for a while before they were all caffeined out and ready to go their separate ways. 'So what are you girls doing now?' asked Les.

Louise shook her head. 'I've got a stack of housework to do. Starting with a pile of washing.'

'I'm going to Bondi Junction and check out the specials,' smiled Jenny. 'What about you, Les?'

'Me,' replied Les. 'I might go down and check out the Bondi Markets.'

'Not a bad way to spend Sunday afternoon,' said Louise. 'I wish I was going with you.'

They paid the bill then stepped outside and went their separate ways. The girls walked up to Six Ways, where Louise had left her car. Les strolled down Hall Street towards Campbell Parade.

Well, that's a funny one, thought Les, as he neared the Post Office. Some rooster ringing me up out of the blue, telling me where to look for Menny's script. Whoever it is, they know what they're talking about. I wonder if it was Lasjoz? He could have got my number off Menny and the voice had a gravelly, European sound. Deep Throat, smiled Les. That's what I've found myself. A Deep Throat. Yeah. Between Irish John and Deep Throat, you can bet I'll finish up in more deep shit. Les joined the Sunday push along Campbell Parade and walked down to Bondi Beach Public School.

For a cloudy day, the markets were in full swing, with no shortage of casually dressed punters looking for bargains. Les tended to avoid the place because of the crowds. But now and again he'd pop in to buy a T-shirt, a book or some CDs and it was always a good perv. He stepped through the school gate and joined the throng meandering past stalls selling designer and recycled clothes, paintings, bric-a-brac, body oils, sunglasses, all types of jewellery, Tibetan prayer flags, Laotian fisherman's pants, miniature musical instruments, hip flasks, and T-shirts with anyone on the front from Che Guevara to the Three Stooges. Or cryptic messages such as VOTE PEDRO or EVERYTHING BEGINS WITH E. Next to a tent offering Thai massage, Les stopped at a stall selling badges and buttons. A yellow one saying I'M NOT REAL SMART BUT I CAN LIFT HEAVY THINGS caught his eye. Just what I need for work, smiled Les. He paid the bloke and put it in his pocket.

Les drifted up to the stalls at the back selling secondhand goods. He found umbrellas, shoes, toys, kettles, toasters, rolling pins and an assortment of junk you'd probably get cheaper in an op shop. There were backpacks and handbags. But the only green bag was an old vinyl thing with a loose clasp. He checked the stalls thoroughly then looked for the woman that did tarot readings.

Les found her sitting in a small clearing under a tree at a fold-up table covered by a blue cloth. She had a friendly, studious face and straight brown hair, and had on a black top under a loose-fitting blue shirt. A pair of glasses sat halfway down her nose and a gemstone necklace rested across her top. She was on her own, idly shuffling a well-worn set of tarot cards. Les caught her eye and walked up to the empty chair in front of her.

'G'day,' said Les. 'All right if I sit down?'

'Please do,' offered the woman.

Les sat down and shuffled the chair a little closer to the table. 'My name's Les.'

'Hello, Les. I'm Rose,' smiled the woman.

Les waited a moment. 'What do you know about a green bag, Rose?'

The woman's smile disappeared and she tilted her head up to fix Les through her glasses. 'What?'

'A green bag with a black eagle on the side. I was told you might know something about it.'

Rose looked at Les as if he'd just walked into her house and across her carpet with dog shit all over his shoes. 'Are you all right?' she said.

'Yeah. I'm fine,' replied Les.

'Are you a policeman?'

Les shook his head. 'No. Not at all.'

'Do you work with my son at the brewery?'

'No. I . . . work at the Cross.'

'Well, I don't know what you're talking about.' The woman picked up a brown tapestry bag from near her feet and put it on the table. 'There. That's my bag,' she said, then pointed to the cards and the sign above her saying TAROT READINGS. 'And do I look like I deal in bags? she asked.

Les felt like a complete idiot. 'I'm really sorry, Rose,' he blurted. 'I've ... I've got you mixed up with someone else.' Les got up to leave, then hesitated. 'Hey, while I'm here. Why don't you give me a tarot reading?'

'I charge fifteen dollars,' said the woman, placing her bag back at her feet. 'Have you got any money — Les, is it?'

'That's right,' nodded Les. 'Yeah I got money, Rose. Heaps.' Les pulled a healthy roll of fifties and twenties out of his pocket. 'Do you want me to pay you now?'

'No. That's all right,' said Rose. She pushed the cards across to Norton. 'Okay, Les. Shuffle the cards.'

'Righto.'

Automatically, Les shuffled the cards like they did at work. He flicked them around, cut them several times and handed them back to Rose.

'I see you've done that before, Les,' smiled Rose. She had a soothing manner and Les began to feel less uncomfortable as she took the cards.

'Yeah. I play a bit of manilla at a friend's house,' he replied.

'All right, Les,' said Rose. 'We'll just do a six card read. Pick six cards.' Carefully Les did what he was told. 'Now put them down on the table like a cross.' With Rose directing him, Les again did what he was told. 'How long since you've had a tarot reading?' asked Rose, putting the remaining cards to one side.

'I've never had one,' answered Les.

'Well. Different readers have different interpretations. But I'll give you my interpretation. I've been told I'm fairly accurate.

Okay. Let's see what you've got here.' Rose turned the cards over in the order Les had placed them on the table. She studied them for a few moments, and raised her eyebrows.

'All right, are they?' asked Les. 'I'm not going to get run over by a bus, am I? Or hit by lightning?'

Rose slowly shook her head. 'No. Not at all. Actually this is a very interesting spread. I can't remember ever seeing one like this.'

'Oh?' Les stared blankly at the coloured figures on the cards. Rose tapped a card in the middle. 'This is the Hierophant. You search for things. You've got an open mind. You take on quests. You can solve things.'

'Yeah. Fair enough,' said Les. 'People tell me I would have made a good copper.'

Rose tapped another card. 'This is the Tower. It means change. Be prepared. You're going to have to open many strange doors. So expect the unexpected.'

Les looked at the card. It was a bit worn. But he could make out a tower being hit by lightning and two people jumping out of a window. 'I can dig that,' said Les.

'This is the Seven of Swords,' said Rose, tapping the next card 'You have to walk different paths. And someone could be offering you help or advice. Listen to them.'

'Okay,' nodded Les.

Rose tapped another card. 'This is the Seven of Wands. You've got a lot of inner strength. You're able to do your own thing. Mentally and physically.'

'Fair enough,' said Les.

'This is the Six of Cups. You'll meet an old friend. Or an aquaintance. And something old.' Rose shook her head. 'This card's a little odd in comparison to the others.'

'Whatever,' shrugged Les.

Rose tapped the last card for moment more than the others. 'Eight of Pentacles. Again this shows your inner strength. But there's also something from the past that leads to the future. I'm not sure in what way. But despite your uncanny intuition, you still need guidance.'

Les let Rose stare at the cards for a few moments. 'So what's the story, Rose? I'm a tower of strength, I can get things done. But I need help.'

'Kind of, Les. Yes,' nodded Rose. 'But it's not just the cards. It's the way they fall.'

'Oh?'

'Have you been in some sort of life-threatening situation lately? Have you escaped injury, but others haven't?'

'Funny you should say that, Rose,' answered Les. 'I got offered a lift home the other night and knocked it back. And there was a bad accident. Some people got killed, actually.'

'Right,' nodded Rose. 'And have you been offered an assignment or a request lately to look for something. Like an old painting. Or a book?'

'That's uncanny, Rose. A friend of mine had an old Bible stolen. And he thinks I might be able to find it. He even offered me a small reward.'

'You'll find it, Les. And you will be rewarded.' Rose thought for a moment. 'Although your reward could come from another source.'

'But I'll finish in front?'

'Oh yes. Well in front,' said Rose. 'There could also be a joker in the pack. Misleading you. So expect the unexpected.'

'Okay,' said Les.

'And … I don't know.' Rose stared at the cards a little mystified. 'You're going to find something old.'

'Old?'

'Yes. Really old,' emphasised Rose. 'Ancient. And on a different path.'

'Sounds a little kooky,' said Les.

'Nothing to be afraid of,' said Rose. 'But you will be astonished. You'll also find something else that's old. Not quite as old. Very different to the other.'

'Sounds good to me,' said Les.

'Just be careful, Les. You'll find your desire. And you'll do quite well. But there could be unexpected pitfalls. Show caution. And use your inner strength. The time could come when you may have to dig deep. Very deep.' Rose smiled and put the cards back in the pack. 'So that's it, Les. Good luck. You're a nice man.'

'Thanks, Rose.' Les pulled fifty dollars off his roll and gave it to her. 'Here Rose,' he smiled. 'Take that for me being a bit of dill earlier.'

'You're no dill, Les,' replied Rose, pocketing the money. 'And thank you very much. Come back and tell me what happened. I'm interested.'

'I'll do that. Goodbye. And thanks again, Rose.'

'My pleasure.'

A blonde girl in a thick red shirt and jeans had been waiting patiently. Les stood up and moved the chair around. 'There you go,' he smiled. 'I warmed the seat for you.'

The girl returned Norton's smile.

'Thank you,' she said.

The girl sat down and Rose straightened her glasses. Norton left the markets and walked straight home.

Back inside the house, Les made a mug of herb tea and took it into the loungeroom, leaving the TV and stereo off, preferring to sit in silence. Oh shit, thought Les, as he pensively sipped his hot tea. I'm not rapt in those things. That bloody Rainbow Princess read my runes or something in Cairns and I nearly got eaten by a giant cat, or whatever it was. That wasn't much fun, I can tell you. Les reflected on the blank TV screen and took another sip of tea. But Rose's was different. It was a tarot. It was definitely a bit spooky how she sniffed out those deaths around me and how I was looking for something for someone. But everything else she told me was quite positive. Just watch myself and I'd finish up with the goodies. I'll do quite well. She also said someone would be offering me help and I should listen to them. Les took a slow sip of tea. That could be Deep Throat. Hey. Maybe Deep Throat secretly wanted me to have a tarot reading? Maybe it was all in the cards? Like the joker in the pack. Rose also said I might have to open many strange doors. That makes sense if I'm sneaking around looking for something. And I can't go quietly opening doors with a pair of Doc Martens. For doors you need a key. And, smiled Les, I know just the bloke who can arrange one. Les walked over, picked up the house phone and dialled.

'Hello?'

'Hello, Eddie. It's Les.'

'Les. How are you, mate?'

'All right. Heaps better than I was.'

'Price said you'll be back next week some time.'

'Probably. Hey, that was a nice photo in the paper today.'

'Yeah,' said Eddie. 'I just got out of the road in time.'

'Jesus, he cleaned up.'

'Almost two million. It was the sting of the century.'

'It sure was.'

'So what can I do for you, mate?'

Knowing Eddie disliked talking on the phone, Les got to the point. 'Eddie, I'm looking for something and I need a key. That mate of yours at Rose Bay still in business?'

'He's still in business,' said Eddie. 'But he's moved up to Long Jetty on the Central Coast, to be near his family.'

'The Central Coast. That's all right. I can take a run up.' The Wile E. Coyote light bulb above Norton's head suddenly came on. 'Hey. I might even stay there a couple of nights. Give myself a break from all this noise and pollution. It's not bad up there.'

'In that case,' said Eddie. 'I might be able to do you another favour.'

'You can?'

'Yeah. An old mate of mine's running a big holiday apartment thing at Terrigal. He owes me a favour. I'll see if can I organise a couple of nights for you on the house.'

Les was chuffed. 'Unreal.'

'I'll ring you back in ten minutes.'

Eddie hung up and Les kicked back in the lounge. Well, this is all right, he smiled. I get my master key and a nice little holiday at the same time. I like Terrigal, and being able to do my own thing up there will be absolutely delightful. Les finished his mug of tea and the second ten minutes had passed, the phone rang.

'Hello?'

'Yeah. I've sorted everything out. You got a Biro?'

'Right here, mate. Fire away.'

Eddie gave Les his locksmith mate's details and the details of his other mate who ran the resort.

'You'll like Ocean Star Apartments,' said Eddie. 'They're right across from the ocean. Glen's a good bloke, too. And when you get your key cut, slip Kenny a few extra bucks. His granddaughter needs an eye operation.'

'Good as gold.'

'All right. Have a good time up there, Les. I'll see you when you get back.'

'Okay. Thanks, Eddie.'

Les hung up and took his empty cup out to the kitchen. Well, that's all right, he smiled. A holiday on the house. Les winked up at the sky. You have your moments, don't you, boss. Les checked the addresses and the two names again. Kenny Taylor and Glen Kaplan. I'll leave the locksmith alone. But I'll ring the other bloke just to break the ice. Les picked up the phone and dialled again.

'Hello. Ocean Star. Glen Kaplan speaking.'

'Oh Glen. My name's Les Norton. Did Eddie ring you about me?'

'He sure did.' The voice was warm and friendly. 'What time are you coming up?'

'Depending on the traffic, tomorrow morning before lunch. Is that okay?'

'No problem at all. You know how to get here?'

'Yeah. I've stayed in Terrigal before.'

'Well, we're on the main drag as you pass the Skillion. Just pull into the drive and sound the buzzer.'

'All right. I'll see you in the morning. Thanks, Glen.'

'No worries, Les.'

Glen hung up and Les stared at the phone. There it is. Done deal. And there'll be nothing doing up there early in the week. So I'll just eat, sleep and train. Maybe have the odd cool one. And forget about Sydney. I wonder what the weather'll be like? Les peered out the window. Mmmh. Looks like it's getting ready to rain down here. Les was contemplating what to take with him, when his mobile phone rang. 'Hello?'

'Yes. It's me again. Bodene Menjou's friend.'

'Deep Throat,' said Les.

'Is that what you wish to call me?' said the voice.

'Sure. Why not,' answered Les.

'Very well,' replied the voice. 'Is good. So how did you go down at the Bondi Markets?'

'Well, I didn't find any green bag. And Rose the tarot reader knew nothing. But she gave me a good tarot read.'

'You had your tarot read?'

'I sure did,' said Les.

'Excellent.' Suddenly the voice sneezed violently.

'Gesundheit,' said Les.

'Yeah,' sniffed the voice. 'Something like that. Now, I have somewhere else for you to look.'

'Somewhere else?' said Les.

'Yes. And there could be more. But I want you to find the bag. It is important you do.'

'And all you want is satisfaction,' said Les.

'That is right. Now have you a Biro ready?'

'I have.'

'Excellent. The street runs off Bondi Road and the house is on the right near the end. I believe the bag was left out the front.'

'Out the front?'

'Yes. Look for it there. Here is the address.'

'Righto.' Les wrote down the address and read it back.

'That is good,' said the voice. 'Now I must go. I will ring you back.'

Les placed his mobile on the table and looked at the address. I think I know where that is, he mused. Not far from the Royal Hotel. He looked out the window again. It looks like it's going to rain later, so I may as well go round now. No need to get changed.

But this time I'll wear those gloves I keep in the car for changing flats. Christ! If I'd have known all that shit was going to go down, I would have worn them last night. Be nice if I'd cut myself. There was blood everywhere. Les put the address in the back pocket of his jeans, locked the house then climbed behind the wheel of his car and drove off.

The street wasn't hard to find. It was a short, narrow, one-way thoroughfare running from Bondi Road towards Birrell Street. Les checked the numbers. The house was on the right-hand side near the end, wedged between a small block of units on the right and another house on the left. Les crammed his car against someone's driveway opposite and walked down. He checked the number, checked it again and gave a double blink.

It was a single-storey cottage with a tatty brick fence out the front and no front gate. A small porch with a front door sat on the right-hand corner, next to a weed-infested driveway that led to an overgrown backyard. Beneath a sagging powerline, several leafless trees pushed against the front and side fences. There was no gate to the side passage, the letter box had broken off and most of the guttering had rusted away. Instead of a verandah, a double room full of broken windows faced the street, covered over by a flapping square of thin green tarpaulin, frayed at the edges and full of splits. The old house was the most decrepit, tumbledown dump Les had ever seen. Squatters wouldn't even live in it. But as well as being an absolute eyesore, the whole place was piled with rubbish. In some parts, it was over two metres high. Les stood on the unkempt nature strip, gobsmacked.

There were piles of newspapers, magazines and cardboard. Prams, toys, Boogie Boards, Coolite boards, surfboards, push-bikes, scooters, skateboards and other sports goods all rusted and broken. Paint tins, bottles, jars, shoe boxes, plastic containers, mattresses, cardboard boxes full of tins, broken cardboard boxes spilling out tins and jars half full of stagnant green water, crawling with larvae. Smashed TV sets, broken stereos, old ghetto blasters, plastic bags of vinyl records. You name an article of rubbish that had been thrown out in a street clean-up or dumped on the side of the road and something similar was in there, rusting or rotting away.

Lord have mercy, thought Les. Where do I start? He checked the room facing the street and could perceive no sign of life. Well, I suppose I'd better start by getting my gloves. Les walked back to the car and got a pair of cheap all-purpose leather gloves from the boot. He put them on and adjusted his cap then, just as it began to rain, started searching through the rubbish.

Les was groping around in the filth and stench, dodging cockroaches and millipedes and other horrible crawling bugs and cursing his luck when he uncovered it. Beneath a pile of rotting tea towels. A green handbag with a . . . dinosaur on the side.

'Ahhh shit!' cursed Les, tossing the empty bag aside.

Filth and grime clinging to his rain soaked clothes and trainers, Les searched on amongst the sodden piles of rubbish. A trickle of cold water ran down his neck and he was seriously thinking of giving the whole idea a miss and telling Deep Throat what to do with his instructions the next time he called.

Rummaging away, Les knelt down to upend a pile of rotting underlay and a roll of filthy grey carpet when he sensed movement behind him. Next thing, he felt a sharp pain as someone hit him across the head with something.

'What the fuck!'

Les turned and looked up at a grim, hatchet-faced old woman wearing a plastic raincoat and a blue scarf over her head. She was holding a black plastic garden rake above her which she viciously banged down across his head again.

'Kriminal! Kriminal!' the old woman shrieked as she whacked into Les with the rake handle. 'What you are doing in my belongings, kriminal? Go vay. Go vay, kriminal.'

'Jesus Christ! Piss off will you,' yelled Les, trying to ward off the blows.

Les was slipping and sliding around in the mud and rubbish when two women, a little younger but similar in looks and clothing to the older one, came from the door at the corner of the house and joined in the attack. One had a dust broom, the other a squeeze mop.

'Kriminal. Kriminal,' they shrieked, as they helped the older woman bash into Les. 'Die, kriminal bastard. Die.'

Under a torrent of blows from the three women, Les staggered to his feet and picked up an overnight bag full of stinking wet rags. He hurled it at the younger woman on the left, who screamed as it knocked her on her backside amongst the piles of rubbish. This sent the other two women into an even wilder frenzy.

'Bastard! Bastard!' they spat at Les, furiously raining blows upon him. 'Murdering kriminal bastard. Die, stinking shit bastard.'

'Ohh fuck you,' howled Les. 'Stick your lousy rubbish in your arse.' Les hastily stepped back out of the driveway to the other side of the footpath and stared at the three women in disbelief before beating a retreat to the safety of his car. The three women continued to shriek at him, still brandishing their cudgels.

'Kriminal! Kriminal!' they shouted.

'Go from our street, kriminal!'

'Yes. And doesn't coming back. Bastard!'

'Christ! You needn't worry about that,' said Les, painfully getting back behind the wheel. 'You're off your fuckin heads.'

Les started the car and the wheels spun on the wet road before he sped off, putting as much distance as he could between himself and the three maddened women in the shortest time possible.

Les hung two lefts before he pulled up for the lights at the Royal Hotel and checked himself out in the rear-vision mirror. As well as being soaking wet and covered in filth, there was blood all through his cap and trickles were running down his face and dripping off his chin. Under his top, he could feel welts along his arms and across his shoulders. A family pulled up alongside in a station wagon and they all stared at his condition. Les snarled back at them and roared off down Denham Street when the lights changed, not stopping till he pulled up outside Chez Norton. Checking to see there were no neighbours around, Les dragged his sorry arse out of the car, locked it and went inside.

In the bathroom, Les couldn't believe the dishevelled, bloodied face staring back at him in the mirror. 'Shit! Can I find them or what,' he cursed. 'This is getting to be a bloody habit.'

Les went to the laundry, stripped off and once again threw everything into the washing machine along with plenty of Dynamo and a liberal splash of Pine O Cleen. While that was going round, he got under the shower and let the hot water sting all the cuts as he washed away the dirt and blood. Under closer inspection with a hand mirror, none of the cuts needed stitching, but he was covered in welts and the crazed women had landed a few blows across his jaw and nose. After a long, hot shower, Les ran a bath, added some Dettol and had a good soak while he cursed his luck once more. You hate me, don't you, boss, he grimaced, staring out the bathroom window. I know you do. That's okay, mate. I can handle it. But just tell me the reason. I do have rights, you know.

After getting out of the bath, Les dried off, dabbed some Dettol cream on his cuts and welts, and wrapped a blue check cotton scarf round his head. He changed into a grey, fleecy lined tracksuit, poured himself a delicious and settled down to watch the Sunday football. Brisbane vs Manly — which turned out a pretty good game, with Brisbane getting up at the death, 34–30. Half full of delicious, Les grilled a T-bone which he devoured with brown rice and salad, tea and toast.

Once he'd cleaned up in the kitchen, Les packed a bag with what he thought he'd need in Terrigal, including his Speedos and snorkelling gear. Satisfied he had everything, he dropped some

Panadeine capsules, made a delicious, then settled back in front of the TV with another one of Warren's DVDs, *The 300*.

It wasn't the most boring movie Les had ever watched. But for all the hype, it was up there with them. The whole thing was nothing but a surge of flashing white grins and buffed-up six-packs topped by non-stop macho posturing in leather jockstraps. David Wenham traipsed around looking and sounding like Vincent van Gogh after he cut his ear off. Maybe it was all the paracetamol and delicious topped off by a bad day. But after the two-hundredth severed limb fell to the ground and the hundredth decapitated head rolled away, Les was on the nod. The only brief enlightenment occurred in the temple, when the king's wife stabbed the bloke who porked her behind her husband's back. By golly, thought Les, when he put the DVD away, not much point having a stray root back in old Sparta town. You'd be better off with a copy of *Playboy* and a full hand going alone. Les put his mobile phone on charge, switched off the lights and climbed into bed looking forward to an early night. His last thoughts, after he adjusted the scarf round his head, were — thank Christ I'm getting out of Bondi for a couple of days. Les gave one mighty yawn then blacked out.

Les woke up in fairly good spirits the next morning and rose not long after the sun. Outside a few clouds were still hanging around in the light sou'wester, but the rain had gone, leaving a delightful crispness in the air. He went to the bathroom, took the scarf off and checked himself out. His face had seen better days, and he had welts all over him, however the bleeding had stopped and his clothing had protected him from the worst of the crazed women's attack. He picked up his toothbrush and smiled at himself in the mirror.

'Don't worry, mate,' winked Les. 'You're still a handsome, handsome brute.'

When he finished in the bathroom, Les changed into a fresh pair of jeans, a white Jimmy Buffett T-shirt and a clean pair of AND1 trainers.

He went to the kitchen, put the kettle on and made two toasted cheese sandwiches and a mug of tea. He'd have a bigger breakfast at Terrigal, and Les felt the sooner he got going the better. He cleaned up, put his phone in his backpack, snuck two thousand dollars out from behind the panel in his wardrobe and had a last look around. Satisfied everything was in order, Les locked the house and took his bags out to the car. Ten minutes later Les was on the other side of Bondi Junction heading for the Eastern Distributor.

Traffic was light heading out of Sydney and Les fiddled around with FM radio to get some music and pass the time. After a non-stop barrage of gibberish, ads, and the Eagles playing 'Hotel California' fifteen times in a row, Les changed to AM for news and views. Apart from the usual ABC blandness, all he got was a right-wing shock jock on one station debunking global warming and cheering on the war in Iraq, and two politically correct schlock jocks on another station called Mutt and Jeff or something, trying to be funny. Mutt was trying that hard he was giving himself a strangulated hernia and still getting nowhere. I think the best way to sum those two up, thought Les, when he stopped near Gordon for petrol and the paper, is Mutt talks through his arse and Jeff talks through his nose. As soon as Les paid for his purchases, he pissed the radio off and slipped on a tape. Soon Steely Dan was bopping out 'Cousin Dupree' which cut into Gina Jeffreys's raunchy version of the old Janis Joplin song 'Mercedes Benz'. Before Les knew it, he was on the F3 and it was music all the way to the Central Coast.

Driving along with the music playing, Les reflected on his two previous trips to the Central Coast. The first time he met up with crazy Sophia and kind of had fun getting his brains bonked out. But the second trip when he teamed up with Jimmy Rosewater was sad. Jimmy had too much going for him and was too good-looking to die so young. Turning out to be George Brennan's illegitimate son made it even sadder. But, mused Les, I guess that's the way it goes. One thing for sure, ain't nothing going to happen to me this time. No woman would give me a second look with my head the way it is. And I sure as hell ain't getting into any fights. They can laugh, chaff and poke shit at me, I will not react. I'll get my master key, kick back and relax with a few drinks at wherever it is I'm staying.

Before Les knew it, the Moonee Moonee Bridge was behind him and he was hanging a right at Bluetongue Stadium. He hung another right at Erina Fair into Terrigal Drive, and Alabama 3 were crackling into 'Cocaine Killed My Community' when Les cruised into Terrigal with the ocean on his left.

There'd been some development since Les had been there last, including a row of prestige units on the right. The Flathead Spot had grown and moved next door and there was a new surf club. The road had been narrowed into a one-way strip heading towards the Haven and the footpath on the right was now a wide boulevard full of restaurants with outdoor dining. Les slowed down for the speed humps before coming to a three-way pedestrian crossing where the resort stood on the corner. May as well cruise the rest of the hood, shrugged Les, and hung a right.

The little butcher shop was still next to the fruit shop and there were two more restaurants with bars above overlooking the street. The church was still open for business, but the hardware store was now a gourmet pizza restaurant with a classy looking little bar next door called the Point. Les hung a right at the bank and came down Church Street.

Coffee shops had sprung up everywhere and the punters grouped outside one opposite the police station gave it the appearance of a scene. Les hung another right at the end and found a Subway franchise, and the one-man barber shop opposite the TAB was gone, replaced by a juice bar. Les turned right again at a fish café next to an Italian restaurant sitting alongside the local cake shop, then checked out the water through the towering pine trees. He continued on past the resort where an open-air restaurant facing the beachfront caught his eye, then checked the address again as the road rose past the

Skillion. Where it curved towards the approaching houses and units, he found what he was looking for: Ocean Star Apartments, a spreading complex of clay-coloured units with rounded balconies and bay windows facing the ocean. Les pulled up at a blue wrought-iron gate set in a wide driveway flanked by palm trees and pressed the buzzer.

'Hello?' a voice crackled over the intercom.

'Yeah. Is Glen Kaplan there please?' asked Les.

'Speaking.'

'It's Les Norton. Eddie Salita's mate. I rang you yesterday.'

'Sure, Les. Come straight in. I've been expecting you.'

'Thanks.'

The gate swung open, Les switched off the car stereo and followed a curved driveway past a tennis court to the main entrance where a bank of shimmering glass windows faced a magnificent three-tiered fountain nestled amongst several fat palm trees. He stopped and cut the engine just as a dapper man with short grey hair and a neatly trimmed moustache appeared from behind a glass door wearing a red striped shirt with a button-down collar and jeans. He waited till Les got out of the car and stepped up to him with a friendly smile.

'Les,' he said, offering his hand. 'I'm Glen. The manager.'

'Pleased to meet you, Glen,' replied Les, shaking Glen's hand.

'How was the trip up from Sydney?'

'Good,' nodded Les. He cast an eye around the units and the beautifully landscaped grounds thick with healthy palm trees. 'Crikey. Not a bad spread you've got here, Glen.'

The manager winked. 'You ain't seen nothing yet, mate. Grab your stuff and we'll get you stowed away.'

'Righto.' Les got his bags from the back seat of the Berlina and followed Glen into the lobby. 'Do I have to fill in a form?'

Glen patted Norton's shoulder. 'No. Don't worry about it. You're a special guest.'

'Thanks.'

Les was impressed from the moment he stepped inside. The resort was all class and good taste. Original oil paintings hung along sparkling white walls and stands holding up teak yachts with metal sails reflected off scrupulously polished wooden floors. A tan leather lounge faced the front desk and office where a carved wooden Buddha, decorated with frangipanis, sat near the windows. Everything was softly lit and pleasantly air-conditioned. Glen led Les along a short hallway to an elevator and pushed a button.

'So where do you know Eddie from?' asked Les, as they waited for the lift. 'Through Price?'

Glen shook his head. 'No. I used to live next door to him in Sydney. He did me a couple of favours.'

'Oh?'

'Yes. One of my daughters had a hot-blooded boyfriend who didn't know what adios and goodbye meant. So Eddie had a word with him.'

'And you never saw him again, I presume,' smiled Les.

'No, we didn't,' said Glen. 'In fact no one has, for that matter. Him or his hot-blooded brother.'

'Yes. Eddie's very efficient like that,' said Les.

Glen smiled. 'He tells me you're very efficient at what you do too, Les.'

Before Les had a chance to reply, the lift stopped and he was following Glen down a hallway hung with more oil paintings, till Glen opened a white door numbered eight.

'There you go, Les,' said Glen, moving aside. 'That do you?'

Les stepped inside and gave a double blink. 'Holy shit,' he said. 'Who owns this? The Sultan of Brunei?'

Les dropped his bag in the hall and followed Glen into a huge loungeroom where a caramel-coloured ottoman that would have held a football team sat on ankle-deep white carpet. All around, the apartment was done out in Italian white marble, and next to the lounge was a dining room with a glass table and eight tapestry chairs. Crystal chandeliers tinkled from the ceiling, copper urns filled with artificial flowers sat on glass tables and a stereo and a widescreen TV faced the lounge, while the predominantly white decor was broken by the striking blue of several Brett Whiteleys. Three bedooms ran off the hallways and adjacent to the lounge was a fully equipped, state-of-the-art kitchen. Glen slid open a glass door and allowed Les to step out onto a massive balcony spread with top-of-the-range outdoor furniture and a view that went from the boats in Terrigal Haven to the lighthouse at Norah Head.

'Not a bad view, Les,' said Glen.

'Reckon.' Les pointed to a chain of tankers anchored out to sea. 'What's with all the ships? It looks like the D-day invasion.'

'They're coal loaders,' replied Glen. 'There'd be at least seventy between here and Newcastle waiting to load up.' The manager glanced at a pager on his belt. 'Les. I have to go. I've got twenty Germans arriving any minute.'

He handed Les a key ring with what looked like a small black ceramic crayon attached to it. 'There's the key to the door. The pointer's for the security gate and the garage. Just follow the signs downstairs to the garage.'

'Righto,' replied Les, taking the key ring.

Glen started to move off. 'Anything you want. Give me a bell.'

'Okay. And thanks, Glen. This is . . . I don't know. What can I say?'

'No worries, mate,' winked Glen.

The door opened and closed and Glen was gone, leaving Les to his own devices. He gazed at the view for a few moments then got his bag from the hall and took it into the master bedroom.

Like the rest of the apartment, it was mainly white Italian marble. A queen-size bed with a white duvet sat against one wall, and amongst the plush trappings another Brett Whiteley and a William Dobell faced a bay window with the same view as from the balcony. A sparkling white ensuite ran off the bedroom. Shit. How did I fluke this? Les asked himself as he placed his bag on the bed. I'm going to have to milk Glen for another couple of days. A fortnight would be even better. Les started to unpack, then thought it might be a good idea to move his battered old car from the driveway first; he left his bag and took the lift back to the lobby. Just as he got behind the wheel, a tour bus pulled up behind him and disgorged a party of very sober, very correctly dressed men and women. That's got to be the boxheads, smiled Les, checking them out through his rear-vision mirror. All oudt for extremely serious fun unt games, ja? Les slipped the Berlina into drive and moved off.

Les followed the signs down and came to another gate. He pushed the pointer into a small aperture in the wall and the gate swung open. A little further on he found a three-car garage with the door open and number eight on the wall alongside. Les parked his car and without bothering to lock the garage, caught the lift back up to the lobby and went for a walk around.

A landscaped path edged with lava rock led down to an open-air pool and a restaurant that faced a waterfall splashing down into pool full of golden carp. Les watched several fat carp blowing bubbles amongst the water lillies for a moment, then followed another set of stairs back up to the fountain.

To the right was a cosy snooker room and library hung with spectacular Tim Jones and Bosko surfing photos, taken at Teahupo'o in Tahiti. Les dwelled on a ripper shot snapped inside a filthy four-metre barrel by the mighty Bosko, then left and walked back out round the fountain and past the tennis court. Through a landscaped alcove a glass door led to a fully equipped gymnasium, and a door opposite opened onto a heated indoor pool. Les let himself in and found comfortable wicker chairs and tables on this side of the pool, and life-size Egyptian murals of pharaohs and priests, alongside panels of Egyptian hieroglyphics on the wall opposite. The ceiling above the pool was a thick cobalt blue and dotted with tiny lights that twinkled on and off like stars. This would look something else at night, surmised Les, and was thinking of taking a closer look at the murals, but a woman was using the pool, so rather than look like he was perving on her, Les left the woman to her splashing about and returned to his room.

After pouring himself a glass of cold water from a jug in the fridge, Les took it out on the balcony to enjoy the view again. He drained the glass and was about to finish unpacking his bag, when a rumbling in his stomach reminded Les all he'd eaten that morning were two paltry toasted cheese sandwiches. It was time for something more substantial. He could have eaten in the apartment. But Les decided he'd walk down to the shops, where the open-air restaurant he'd noticed beneath the resort looked all right. Les picked up his backpack and with his faithful green Bugs Bunny cap firmly on his head, caught the lift down to the lobby. He let himself out the security gate, adjusted his sunglasses and strolled happily down to the beach front, exchanging smiles and pleasantries with any passersby.

The restaurant was called Serene's and sat in a half-circle of shops that belonged to the resort. Chairs and tables were set out in the open and there was an indoor dining area and kitchen where a colourful mural of a village scene covered the walls. Les chose a table near the hotel's beer garden and settled down with his morning paper. Several waitresses in black were hovering around the punters at the other tables, including an Asian girl with a flower in her hair and a tall woman with glasses. Les was studying the menu when an attractive waitress with dark brown hair pulled back in an untidy ponytail that had a pair of sunglasses jammed in it, appeared at his table holding a Palm Tec waiter's pad. She had big boobs and a solid backside and the way she stood next to the table seemed to display an aura of haughty insouciance. Les wasn't sure whether it was his perception of the girl's attitude, the trouble she appeared to be having with the electronic waiter's pad, or the smartarse that always came out in him when he wore his Bugs Bunny cap, but Les felt compelled to have a go at her. He watched the waitress vexatiously stabbing the pointer at her waiter's pad for a moment, then closed the menu and looked up.

'Do you happen to work here at all?' sniffed Les, giving the waitress a cavalier once-up-and-down.

The girl took a deep breath. 'No,' she replied indifferently. 'They just pay me to stand around and make the place look good.'

'Yeah? Well you can tell whoever owns the place, they're wasting their money. Now if you're finished talking to your boyfriend on the phone, I'd like to order.'

'It's not a phone,' smouldered the girl. 'It's a . . .' She was about to swear then stopped. 'Palm Tec waiter's pad,' she replied.

'Oh? And do you have to be a rocket scientist to work it, do you?' enquired Les.

'No,' replied the girl. 'You just have to be Jesus Christ to put up with some of the customers. That's all.'

'Oh? Is that right?' said Les.

'Yes,' answered the girl. 'And if you're having trouble reading the menu,' she added with an icy smile, 'we have another inside with big letters and little bunny rabbits and monkeys on it.'

'Really?' said Les. 'Well, while you're on the subject of monkeys, do you mind if I offer you some advice?'

'Not at all, sir,' replied the girl. 'What is it?'

'If you happen to pass a woman in the street with a really nice hairdo, ask her the name of her hairdresser. And if she won't tell you, grab her by the arm and start crying.'

The waitress studied Norton's face for a moment. 'And may I offer you some advice too, sir?'

'Sure,' smiled Les.

'Don't wear that mask when you're out in public. You don't only look stupid, you're scaring the children and making the dogs bark. Now,' she smiled back. 'Would you care to order? Or would you prefer to sit there looking like you just got booted off *Big Brother*?'

'No. I'll have scrambled eggs and bacon on Turkish with grilled tomato, please.'

'Coffee?'

'Yeah. An Al Pacino, thanks.'

'A what?' said the girl.

'Sorry,' apologised Les. 'I forgot. I'm out in the bush. I'll have a latte. And make sure it's in a clean glass.'

'Sorry. But we're fresh out of clean glasses,' apologised the girl. 'How about a dirty one and a piece of newspaper to wipe it with?'

Before Les could reply, the waitress turned and walked off. He continued reading his paper and a few minutes later the girl was back with his latte in one hand and his cutlery wrapped in a serviette in the other.

'If you're curious,' the girl smiled pleasantly, 'the silver things are a knife and fork. You use them to eat with. The fork is the one with the little pointy bits at the end. Any problems,' she purred, 'tell me. And I'll get you a nice big spoony-woonie and a nice little bibby-wib. Okay?'

Again the girl walked off leaving Les with his coffee and paper. Les sugared his coffee and took a sip. Shit! he thought. There's nothing wrong with the coffee. It's the grouse. Les read the paper and by the time the girl came back with his breakfast, he'd finished his coffee.

'There you are, sir. Scrambled eggs and bacon on Turkish. Sorry about the plate,' she smiled. 'But the chef's using the bucket. Someone stole his spittoon.'

'That's okay,' said Les. 'Saves him using your handbag. But you can bring me another latte when you're ready.'

'Coming right up.'

Les watched the girl walk away, then started eating. His food was delicious. The eggs were creamy, the tomato was perfect, the bacon had been crisped on a char grill and the bread was toasted and buttered to perfection. Les ripped in. He was still ripping in when the girl arrived with his coffee.

'Everything all right, sir?' the girl asked, placing Norton's coffee on the table, along with the bill.

'Mmhglihrrf,' Les nodded enthusiastically through a mouthful of food.

'I'll take that as a yes,' she answered.

The girl walked away leaving Les to his meal. He polished it off then lingered over the paper with his coffee. Several punters came and went, the boats bobbed up and down in the sparkling blue waters of the Haven and a flock of screeching seagulls attacked a pile of leftover chips someone had thrown to them near the pine trees. Les finished his coffee, glanced at his watch and decided to make a move. He put his paper back in his bag, picked up the bill and walked over to the register where the girl was standing on her own. She glanced up at Norton's arrival.

'Everything to sir's satisfaction,' she asked, unctuously.

'Absolutely delightful,' replied Les, handing her a fifty.

'Oh I'm so pleased,' said the girl. 'Otherwise my whole day would have been completely ruined.'

Les took his change then fished in the pocket of his jeans and came up with another fifty. 'There you go gorgeous,' he said, handing her the money. 'Buy yourself a new hairbrush. Get four. One for each side of your head.' Before she could reply, Les turned and was on his way. He'd just made it past the first table when a voice called out.

'This better not be counterfeit, Ugly. We've had your type in here before.'

Cursing inwardly, Les tried to ignore her and left the restaurant. So what will I do now? mused Les, as he stood gazing around on the footpath. I could check out the punters in the hood. But it's not getting any earlier, why don't I drive out to Long Jetty and get my key? He put his sunglasses on and followed the hill back to the resort.

Les didn't bother going into his apartment. Instead he went straight down to the garage, got his car and headed off out the main gate. Now, if I remember right, Long Jetty is on the way to The Entrance, he told himself. So if I go back the way I came in, I should get there okay. Les switched the tape deck on and with Marcia Ball hollering 'Louella', did a victory lap of Terrigal via the police station then drove past the hotel opposite the lagoon and headed for Erina Fair and the roundabout onto The Entrance Road.

Before long Les had passed Forresters Beach and Bateau Bay Village. Then the road narrowed and it was all shops and business outlets on either side. Les checked the address on the piece of paper next to him. He went past Tuggerah Lakes RSL and an old hall further on, before he found what he was looking for on the opposite side of the road, between a surf shop and a hairdresser. Taylor's Hardware and Paint. Keys Cut. Gas Bottles Filled. Les waited for the traffic, did a U-turn then pulled up out the front and cut the engine.

The front window was written over with whatever specials were on offer and in an alcove on the right, another window with less sign writing sat next to a fly-screen door. Les got out of the car, walked over and stepped inside. Along one wall were cans of paint, brushes, rollers and buckets, etc. Tables of paint and other items sat in the middle and on the other wall were gardening tools, rakes, pinch bars, drills, electric chainsaws and so forth.

The counter was down the back with the cash register at one end and a paint mixer at the other.

Standing in the middle, wearing a grey dust coat, was a tall man with a long face and untidy black hair going grey. A pair of dark eyes set deep beneath his forehead seemed to say he'd seen it all, and a pair of glasses hung on a plastic chain round his neck. He looked up impassively as Les approached.

'Yeah. What can I do for you, mate?' he asked quietly.

'Are you Kenny Taylor?' asked Les.

'I could be. Who wants to know?'

'My name's Les Norton. I believe Eddie Salita rang you about me yesterday.'

'Ahh yes. You're the man who wants a zinger. How are you, Les. I'm Kenny.'

'Nice to meet you, Kenny,' said Norton, shaking the offered hand. 'So what is it you just said I needed?' Les asked.

'A zinger,' replied Kenny. 'That's what I call my version, anyway. Wait here a sec.'

The owner disappeared through a door at the back and returned with a small black plastic box, longer, but half as wide as, a cigarette packet.

He placed it on the counter and flicked it open. Inside was a shiny stainless-steel object resembling a small torch. There was a black button on the top and at one end was a thin, shiny steel rod, flattened and serrated at the point. Kenny took the metal object out of the plastic box and placed it on the counter.

'So that's a zinger,' said Les. 'What's it do?'

'I suppose you've seen those secret-agent movies, Les,' answered Kenny, 'where one of Charlie's Angels or whoever jiggles a thing in a lock and the door pops open.'

'Yeah,' nodded Les. 'But they didn't look like that.'

'No. Because half of those things are bullshit. They do work, but mostly on one brand of lock. This opens the lot.' Kenny picked up the zinger, slid his finger along the steel rod and opened a small aperture on the side. 'Mine works on a titanium oscillator and two A4 batteries. See?' Les had a look and nodded before Kenny closed the aperture. 'What it does, it dislodges the pins inside the lock. Takes seconds at the most.'

'Right,' nodded Les.

Kenny pressed the black button and the steel rod vibrated strongly, making a quiet, ringing sound. 'All you do is poke the oscillator in the keyhole and keep your finger on the button till you hear the pins click. Then push the door open. Sometimes you might have to turn a latch. But that's all. Here,' said Kenny, switching off the zinger. 'You have a go.'

Les took the zinger and pressed the button at the back. He ran it for a moment or two, then took his finger off the button and handed it back to Kenny. 'Looks all right to me, Kenny,' said Les. 'What do I owe you?'

'Seven hundred and fifty bucks,' replied the locksmith, placing the zinger back in its plastic box.

Les fished a roll of hundreds from his jeans and slid them across the counter. 'Why don't we make it a thousand, and call it square.'

'Thanks very much, Les,' said Kenny, transferring the money to a pocket in his dust coat. 'And if anybody should ask you, you never got it from me. Okay?'

'If anybody should ask,' replied Les, 'they'll get the same answer they always get. I got it off a bloke down the pub. And he didn't tell me his name.'

'Lovely.' Kenny looked behind Les, and Les turned to see an elderly lady in a blue dress with grey hair and thick glasses approach the counter. 'Hello, Mrs Bennett,' said Kenny. 'How can I help you?'

'I need a couple more keys cut, Ken,' said the woman.

'I'll do them for you right now,' replied Kenny.

Les picked up the black plastic box. 'I'll get going, Kenny. Thanks for that.'

'No worries, Les. Nice doing business with you.'

Les exited the shop then got back in his car and headed for Terrigal. Shit. How good's this thing? he smiled, as he passed the RSL. Apart from doing break-ins, couldn't you have some fun with it. Like getting square with those two narks across the road who're always whingeing about everything from Warren parking his car to Mrs Curtin's old cat. I could sneak into their house when they're out and drop a big steaming Henry in the loungeroom. Wouldn't that give them something to whinge about. Les was so engrossed in the potential of his new toy, he didn't even bother to turn the stereo on and before he knew it, he was back at the resort and the car was in the garage.

Les was whistling softly when he got out of the lift and walked down the hallway to his apartment. He was about to put the key in the door then stopped. Yeah, why not? Les put the key back in his pocket and got the plastic box from his bag. He removed the zinger, poked the oscillator in the keyhole and pushed the button. There was the familar faint ring, followed by the sound of pins rattling. Les removed the zinger, turned the handle and the door swung open. Well how about that, smiled Les. He put the zinger back in his bag, walked inside to his room and finished unpacking.

When he'd finished, Les poured himself a glass of water and took it out onto the balcony. It was a beautiful warm day and, across the road, the water in Terrigal Haven looked blue and inviting. The boats were still rocking gently at their moorings and a flock of pelicans were either paddling about in the water or waddling around on a small beach in front of a dive centre sitting beneath a restaurant and a coffee shop. Les finished his glass of water, then changed into a pair of shorts and thongs, put his snorkelling gear in his bag and headed for the Haven.

Les spent a delightful afternoon snorkelling. The cool water felt good on his cuts and he saw several stingrays, a few blackfish and whiting and found a rusted old watch when he was diving up and down amongst the boats. He dried off then strolled down to the Flathead Spot and had an excellent feed of fish and chips, which he washed down at a table out the front with a crisp salad and a bottle of ginger beer. On the way home, a little blonde with a cute backside working in the local cake shop caught his eye, along with an Italian restaurant next door called Eudosia's. Les checked the restaurant's menu and thought he might have dinner there. He stopped at the bottle shop and got some Gentleman Jack, Hahn and mineral water then got a pleasant smile from an attractive woman wearing glasses when he bought a copy of *New Dawn* at the newsagent's. Walking past Serene's, Les couldn't see the cheeky waitress from earlier in the day.

Back in his apartment, Les wasted no time putting his booze in the fridge before opening a bottle and taking it out on the sundeck with his magazine. Three beers later Les was reading an article called 'The Tao of Detox' when the peace and quiet, the luxury of his surroundings and the old drinking-beer-in-the-sun syndrome caught up with the big Queenslander, and he dozed off.

The sun was long gone and there was a slight chill in the air when Les came to life. A little puzzled at first, he blinked and stared over the balcony at a beautiful sight. All the ships waiting to load up now had their lights on, and in the soft darkness looked like a necklace of glittering jewels strung across the horizon. Les gazed at the lights for a while, then stood up, stretched and went inside. After switching on the lights, he tuned the stereo to some local FM and had a shower and a shave. Now wide awake, Les wrapped a towel around himself, poured a delicious and sipped it while he changed into his jeans and a dark blue polo shirt with a denim collar. The first delicious left Norton with a delightful glow, so he had another followed by a beer, which he took out onto the balcony to watch the ships again. By the time he'd finished his beer, Norton's stomach was growling ferociously. So he got into his black bomber jacket and left the resort for the short walk to the restaurant, stopping at the bottle shop for two long necks.

Being early in the week, there weren't many people around. But Eudosia's was doing good business. A tall, dark-eyed waitress found Les a good table in the Perspex-sheltered section on the street, and Les settled down with a beer to peruse the menu. He went for bruschetta, spaghetti frutta di mare for an entree, lamb cutlets Eudosia's for a main, and insalata verde on the side.

The bruschetta arrived and was delightful with dried tomato, Spanish onion and cheese topping. The spaghetti had a nice seafood mix in a red garlic sauce and the cutlets, topped with red capsicums, mushrooms, garlic and red wine sauce, were grilled to perfection. Norton ripped in, washing everything down with chilled beer, before finishing with an eye-popping macchiato. There was even a little light entertainment on the night. Some well-dressed older bloke, who looked like he had money, was inside having dinner with a good-looking girl in tight jeans half his age. After enquiring from the waitress, Les found out the girl wasn't the bloke's daughter. She was his date, and she'd brought her four-year-old daughter along. The girl seemed to know everybody in the restaurant, leaving the sugar daddy with the daughter who absolutely hated him. Les had to laugh at the older bloke crammed into a small section of table surrounded by colouring-in books, crayons, texta colours and dolls, trying his best to eat while the little girl whined for her mother and splattered him with food. The trio finally left the restaurant with the young spunk pushing a stroller, the little girl inside it putting on a raging, screaming, temper tantrum, while the sugar daddy dragged his sorry arse behind, after picking up the tab and getting screamed at and sprayed with spaghetti sauce for his trouble. Poor bastard, laughed Les. I can think of better ways to spend a night out than that. More than happy with his Monday night, Les paid the bill then strolled back the way he came.

After a snooze, a few drinks and a good meal, Les wasn't all that keen to go straight home and settle down in front of the TV. A quiet drink or three would be nice; he headed for the beer garden at the resort.

Although it was short on customers, the beer garden was spacious and nicely laid out with plenty of chairs and tables, two pool tables under a canopy and a giant TV screen showing rugby union. The lounge inside was roomy and spread with more TV sets, an open fireplace, comfortable lounges, bench tables and stools and surfing photos on the walls. Several punters were watching MTV and more were in the adjacent games room, feeding the pokies. Les stepped across to the bar and ordered a double JD and soda. It arrived from a lone barmaid in black and Les thought he might take it outside, half watch the football and just sit and think how sweet it is; staying in a million-dollar apartment for free, with plenty of dollars in his pocket. And more days to come, away from the smog and ratbaggery of Sydney. He was walking past a red lounge tucked away on the right when he heard a girl's voice.

'Hey, Ugly. I thought I told you take that mask off. Don't you know, you look like an idiot.'

Les turned slowly to his right. It was the waitress from Serene's, seated comfortably on the lounge with another girl. But she looked a lot different. She had make-up on, her thick brown hair was shining and combed loosely round her shoulders, and she was wearing a smart black leather jacket with a Mao collar over a tight blue top bursting with cleavage and tucked into a pair of black Levis. The girlfriend had a pretty face with dark eyes and soft lips emphasised by just the right amount of make-up. Her thick dark hair was roughly parted in the middle and she was wearing a cream Levis jacket and a silver and brown top, tucked into a pair of brown Levis. Like the waitress, she was sporting plenty of cleavage but had a tighter rump.

'Well, I'll be buggered,' smiled Les. 'If it isn't Miss Congeniality herself. What brings you out tonight in swinging downtown Terrigal?'

'I was hoping to run into a dreamboat like you,' the waitress purred through a cloud of cigarette smoke. 'And I have. Now my life is complete.'

'Well,' shrugged Les. 'Some girls just have all the luck, don't they.'

The waitress nodded to an empty chair at an adjacent table. 'Pull up a seat and join us,' she said. 'Can you handle a bit of fast company?'

'I can only try,' replied Les. 'Thanks.' Norton placed a seat in front of their lounge and sat down. 'Anyway. I'm Les.'

The waitress fluttered her eyes. 'Well, hi there, Les,' she said. 'I'm Carol. And this is Marla.'

'Hello Carol. Hello Marla,' smiled Les, shaking both their hands. 'Nice to meet you girls.'

'Nice to meet you too, Les,' said Marla.

Marla's eyes were swimming lazily around in her attractive face and somehow Les sensed an immediate good vibe coming his way.

'So what happened to your Woody Allen?' asked Carol. 'You look like you've been lion taming without a whip.'

'Give me a break,' said Les. 'My melon's not that bad.'

'Not that bad? Shit. Don't they have mirrors where you live?'

Les looked evenly at her, then had to smile. 'All right. I got into a fight with a couple of blokes over a parking spot. And one hit me with a squash racket.'

Marla winced and placed her hand on Norton's knee. 'Oh, you poor man,' she said.

'Thanks, Marla. It's nice to know someone's got a little kindness in their heart around here.'

Carol gave Les a quick once up and down. 'Going by the look of you, I'd say you were able to take care of yourself.'

'Yes,' Les replied slowly. 'I managed to deal with the two villains most effectively. And I'm sure that in the future they will think twice before attacking decent citizens going innocuously about their business.'

'In other words,' said Carol. 'You kicked the fuckin shit out them.'

'Yeah, Carol,' nodded Les. 'You could say that. And with a pair of ten-hole fuckin Doc Martens.'

'Well, good for you, Les,' said Marla.

'Thanks, Marla,' replied Norton.

Les had a hefty swallow of Jack Daniel's then got into a shout and some pleasant conversation with the two girls. They both lived with their parents at Wamberal, not far away. Carol worked part-time at the restaurant and was doing a TAFE course in computers. The reason she was so good at putting shit on customers was because the woman that owned Serene's used her as a Rottweiler. If any customers started putting on dramas like whingeing about nothing being good enough and practically wanting you to hold their hand while they were eating, she'd sic Carol onto them. And when they complained about Carol's attitude, the owner would make a big show of sacking Carol in front of them. This kept the customers happy, it kept the boss happy and it kept Carol happy, because she never got the sack and could blissfully continue putting shit on annoying customers. And there was never any shortage, particularly amongst the wide range of tourists visiting Terrigal. She lived at home because she was saving her money to take a trip to America and Europe, and was seeing a panel beater who was away in Coffs Harbour on a fishing trip.

Marla edited children's books. She'd written a couple and done a few stints on radio talking about books. She was handy with a video camera and hoping to get into TV. She recently did a doco on NBN about handicapped children that went over well, and was looking forward to bigger things. She'd been going out with a car dealer named Milton, but broke it off because he was too much of an idiot. So was his family.

Les told them he owned two motels in Sydney and was having a quick holiday in Terrigal. He'd been married. But a year ago, a drunk driver killed his wife on a pedestrian crossing.

'Oh you poor man,' said Marla. 'How awful.'

'Yes,' nodded Les, looking into his drink. 'It wasn't easy. But although Veronica will always have a place in my heart, the grieving period is over. And life must go on.'

'You're so brave,' sympathised Marla, gently placing her hand on Norton's knee.

'I had to be,' smiled Les. He took a sip of bourbon. 'Anyway. Let's change the subject. What brings you out on a Monday night? There's not much doing.'

'We're going to an industrial night at the Point,' said Carol.

'The Point?' queried Les. 'Is that the bar next to the pizza restaurant?'

'That's it,' nodded Marla.

'And what's an industrial night?' asked Les.

'They put one on every third Monday night,' said Carol. 'They're for shift workers. Nurses, doctors. People in the hospitality trade. Or don't have to get up the next day. They drop the prices and everybody goes for it.'

'Carol's not working tomorrow,' said Marla. 'And I've got a rostered day off. So we're going up for a rave. Why don't you come with us?'

'Okay,' said Les. 'I will. Thanks.'

'You're going to have to take the mask off first,' said Carol. 'You do realise that?'

'Yeah. But if I take the mask off, I'll have to take the wig off, too. They come as a set.'

'I have to go the loo,' said Marla. 'I'll be back in a sec.'

Les eased back to let her out and watched her walk off. 'Your friend Marla's nice,' he said. 'Very friendly.'

'Yeah,' nodded Carol. 'She had a pill earlier. Otherwise she probably wouldn't talk to you if you were the last bloke left in Australia.'

'Oh I don't know,' said Les. 'I reckon I'm a bit of a cool swinger.'

Carol gave Les a steady once up and down. 'Do you have a pill now and again, Les?'

Norton shook his head. 'No. I don't mind smoking pot. I tried snorting coke, but the bubbles got caught in my nose. And every time I drop acid, all it does is burn holes in my shoes.' Les finished his drink. 'You want another one, Horseface?'

Carol went for her purse. 'It must be my shout.'

'I'll get them,' said Les. 'Save your money for another facelift. The last one only took the wrinkles out of your kneecaps.'

Les got up and ordered three more bourbons. When he returned, Marla was back from the Ladies and it was Carol's turn.

'You don't smoke, Marla?' asked Les, as Carol walked off.

Marla shook her head. 'No thank you. Seventy bucks a week to give yourself emphysema doesn't sound like a very good investment to me.'

'Yeah,' acknowledged Les. 'That's one way of putting it. Carol doesn't mind a puffer, though.'

'Carol would eat a tobacco sandwich.'

'Did you ever see a movie called *Thank You For Smoking*?' asked Les.

Marla tossed back her head and laughed. 'Oh, that was so funny. Especially when they kidnapped that bloke and coated him with nicotine patches.'

Les and Marla joked about the movie till Carol rejoined them, then they lightly talked about different things till Carol looked at her watch. 'Why don't we go when we finish these?' she suggested.

'Suits me,' said Les.

'Okay.' Marla gave Les a smile. 'Are you going to have a dance with me, Les?' she asked.

Les looked deeply into Marla's eyes. 'Marla,' he said, 'there ain't a man big enough to stop me, or a chain strong enough to hold me back.'

'I like you, Les,' said Marla.

'You're not bad yourself, Marla,' smiled Les.

They finished their drinks then left the hotel for the short walk up to the Point.

From the street, a glass door in an alcove next to the pizza restaurant opened on the right into a short enclosed verandah that went past tables and stools to an open glass door that led into the bar. Behind the alcove was another dining area, and standing at a rail in the alcove was a cheerful, solid bloke with spiky black hair, wearing a black, zip-front security jacket. He smiled as soon as he saw Carol, who smiled back before planting a big kiss on his cheek.

'Hello, Jim darling,' she said sweetly.

'Carol. How are you, sweetheart?' replied the doorman, returning her kiss.

'Good. I got two friends with me.'

The doorman checked Norton's bruised face and rugged appearance for a moment, but noticed he was dressed well and in a good mood. 'No problem,' Jim said, cheerfully. 'Go straight in.'

'Thanks, Jim,' said Carol.

'Good on you, mate,' smiled Les, as they walked past.

Les followed Carol and Marla along the verandah where the punters seated at the stools and tables alongside the windows were sucking on a variety of cigarettes, as if they were expecting a tobacco famine. Les stepped inside the bar and stopped behind Carol and Marla, who had stopped for the people milling around inside. Les peered over their shoulders to check things out. The bar was very contemporary and carpeted in blue with a blue ceiling, and a false ceiling beneath that radiated soft lighting. A long red lounge and a number of stools and tables ran around the wall on the right and an equal number of stools and tables ran along the wall on the left beneath two large mirrors reflecting back at each other. A well-stocked bar stood down the end and on the right was a console, where a blond-haired DJ wearing glasses and a blue Hawaiian shirt was pumping out ambient house music. Although it was cool outside, the place was hot and packed with happy punters; some wearing silly hats and sunglasses, and all having a great time.

'Shit! The joint's going off,' said Les. 'I wasn't expecting anything like this on a Monday night in beautiful downtown Terrigal.'

'Not bad eh?' said Carol.

Les was about to reply when he spotted something at the bar that made him smile. 'Yeah. It's good,' he said. 'Listen. I'll get the first drinks. Same again?'

The girls nodded in unison.

'Okay. See if you can find some stools.'

Les eased himself through the punters towards the bar. Even though there was no dancefloor, it didn't stop the crowd and Les had to duck beneath several madly flailing arms and step around a lot of wild footwork. There were several punters at the bar and Les waited patiently while the two bar staff worked flat out. On the right was a big young Island boy with close-cropped hair, smiling white teeth and a square jaw, wearing jeans and a tight-fitting black T-shirt. On the left was a good-looking, well-stacked brunette in a white shirt and a red tie. It was Houston. The girl who'd been working on Neville Nizegy's yacht when Les was involved with the Murrumbidgee Mud Crabs. Eventually it was Norton's turn.

'Yes. What would you like?' the girl asked.

'I don't know, Spare One. What's good in this joint?' asked Les.

'Patooties,' squealed Houston, when she realised who it was. 'What are you doing up here?'

'I don't know, Spare One,' replied Les. 'I might ask you the same thing.'

'I moved up here. Got married. Had a kid. I've turned into a boring old housewife, Tooties. It's ridic.'

'That's one thing you'll never be, Spare One,' said Les. 'Boring. But I'm up here on a quick holiday.'

'You'll have to come back when it's not so busy,' said Houston. 'We've got our rings hanging out tonight.'

'Fair enough,' nodded Les. 'Anyway. Give me three Jackie's and soda. Ice and slice.'

'Coming right up, Tooties.'

Over the noise, Les and Houston had a quick chat about Nizegy and other things. She introduced him to the barman, whose name was Pete, who found time to shake Norton's hand and wish him the best.

'All right, Spare One,' said Les, after he'd paid for the drinks. 'I'll see you before the night's out and I might call back tomorrow night.'

'Do that, Tooties,' smiled Houston. 'It's always good to see a friendly face. Even the rough ones.'

Like a tightrope walker crossing Niagara Falls, Les shuffled back through the gyrating punters with the drinks on a small plastic tray. The girls had managed to find a table and stools near the entrance. Les placed the drinks on the table and sat down.

'Well. Here's looking up your old address,' he said, clinking his glass against Marla's and Carol's. Les took a sip and gave a double blink. 'Shit. They're not bad bloody drinks.'

'Yeah. They look after you in here,' agreed Carol, hoofing into hers.

'I'm glad I don't have to get up tomorrow,' said Marla.

After that the night went swimmingly. They put away plenty of delicious. Marla was all Norton's way and they had a few jigs in and around the other punters swarming through the bar. And Carol met a solid, fair-haired, ex-army bloke, Piers, who was now a builder and a good mate of Pete the barman, who'd also been in the army. Piers sat with them and joined in a few shouts and Les was glad for the extra company, enjoying Piers' stories about serving in Timor.

The only uneasy incident on the night was when Les noticed Marla staring apprehensively at something happening out the front that was reflected in the mirror opposite their table. Jim the doorman was arguing with a group of four men. The one doing the most arguing was a tall, sallow-faced man with thinning brown hair, wearing a red Holden Racing Team jacket. Next thing Pete left the bar and ducked through a side door leading into the smaller dining area. Piers saw Pete hurrying out, excused himself and joined the doorman and the big barman. The four men doing the arguing were full of themselves when Jim was on his own. But the minute Pete and Piers arrived on the scene, their confidence soon waned and they left.

'Everything all right?' Les asked, when Piers returned to their table.

'Yeah. Just a bunch of yobs full of piss and attitude,' replied Piers. 'Jim wasn't going to let them in.'

'The one in the red jacket was Barry. My ex-boyfriend Milton's brother. He's a prize idiot. So are his mates.'

'Well, they won't be coming in here tonight,' said Piers.

'Good,' replied Marla.

The night continued. Carol kept inching towards Piers and Marla was up against Les, surreptitiously taking his inside thigh measurement. Midnight came and went and although it was non-smoking in the bar, the punters on the verandah were making up for lost time and the fumes were swirling back inside. Besides that, the ambient house music was starting to lose its ambience and Les would have given his left nut to hear Jerry Lee Lewis doing a duet with someone. Anyone — from Barry Manilow to Nana Mouskouri. Marla was nestled up against him and he put his arm around her shoulder.

'Marla,' said Les. 'I hate to be a lemon, but I don't know if I can take much more of this. That music is starting to give me GBH of the earhole. And the smoke's making my eyes feel like I'm blinking fish hooks.'

'Yes. I know what you mean,' agreed Marla.

'Don't take this the wrong way, but would you like to come back to my place and have a drink? I've got some Jackie's and that.'

'I'd love to come back to your place,' smiled Marla. 'I've always wanted to see inside Ocean Star Apartments. They say it's very nice. What's your room like?'

'My room? Oh, it's reasonable enough,' replied Les. 'Could do with a lick of paint. But it hasn't got a bad view.'

'All right,' said Marla. 'I'll tell Carol what's happening.'

'You don't mind catching a taxi home?' said Les. 'Christ! If I blew into a bag, the ocean would catch fire.'

'No. That's okay.'

Les eased back while Marla had a confab with Carol. Before long Marla found her handbag and stood up at the table. Les joined her.

'Well, I don't suppose I'll be seeing you for breakfast tomorrow, Carol,' he said. 'Shit. Who's going to insult me?'

'Oh, I'm sure you'll find somone,' smiled Carol. 'With your head, Knackers, you can't miss out.'

Les reached across and shook Piers's hand. 'Nice to have met you, Piers,' he said sincerely. 'You people did a great job up there in East Timor. Hey. They're still doing a great job everywhere.'

Piers returned Norton's handshake. 'Thanks, Les,' he said. 'I appreciate that. If you got time before you go back, look me up and we'll have a drink.'

'Sounds good to me,' said Norton.

Les and Marla eased their way out the door and through the punters along the verandah. They said goodbye to Jim, and Les thanked him again for letting him in. Jim said it was a pleasure and he was glad they had a good night. They crossed the street and when they got to the resort corner, Les stopped and sucked in a huge lungful of air.

'Oh Marla,' he breathed. 'What about this fresh air. It's full of oxygen.'

'I know what you mean,' she replied. 'I'll have to wash my hair with sugar soap before I go to bed. As for my clothes, I think I'll just burn them.'

They shuffled along arm in arm when something lying on the ground caught Norton's eye. 'What's . . .?' Les picked it up. It was a red, white and blue plastic glasses case with LE SPECS LE TOUGH printed on the side. Les opened the case and inside were a pair of chrome Elvis Presley style sunglasses. 'Holy shit,' cried Les. 'Check these out. Somebody must have dropped them on the way to the Point.' Les couldn't whip them out of the case and put them on quick enough. He turned towards the Point Bar and cupped his hands around his mouth. 'Hey,' Les called out. 'Elvis has left the building. All right?'

'Shit. Carol would kill for those,' laughed Marla. 'She loves Elvis.'

Les threw an arm out and started boozily gyrating one leg. '*You went nuttin' with a ground hog*,' he sang flatly.

'Jesus. Don't ever give up your day job, Les,' Marla advised him.

Laughing away, Les punished Marla with a bit more Elvis on the way up the street, and arm in arm they danced happily around the corner. Suddenly Marla stopped. Sprawled along an empty cab rank outside the resort were the four men Jim wouldn't let into the bar. The one in the red jacket was seated at the end closest to Les and Marla. His three mates, wearing tracksuits, jeans, zip-front jackets and baseball caps, were slouched alongside him. As soon as the one in the red jacket spotted Marla, his face soured into an expression of pure rancour.

'Well, look who it ain't,' he sneered. 'The beautiful Marla. How are you, you fuckin moll.'

Marla rolled her eyes shut for a brief moment. 'Oh Barry,' she pleaded. 'Why can't you just leave me alone?'

'Ohh well, why don't you go and get an AVO on me too,' sniggered Barry. 'You do a lousy TV doco and you think you're too good for my brother. You stuck-up bitch.'

Barry's mate at the end with his hood up decided to put his head in. 'Hey, check out fuckin Elvis,' he laughed.

'Yeah. Where's your blue suede shoes, Elvis?' mocked his mate next to him, wearing jeans and a brown jacket.

Marla gripped Norton's arm and went to walk past the four men. 'Come on, Les,' she said, quietly. 'Don't take any notice of them. They're idiots.'

'Idiots,' said Barry. 'Who are you calling an idiot? You snooty moll.'

The four men rose up from the seat and stood in front of Les and Marla, blocking their way. Barry was closest to a car parked by the footpath. The bloke with the hood up was next to him. Les let go of Marla and stared down at the footpath through his sunglasses as if he was looking for an answer. If he was, it didn't take long for him to find one.

'Barry,' said Les, shaking his head. 'I haven't got the time, nor the patience for this fuckin shit. I really haven't.'

Having said that, Les snap-kicked Barry in the solar plexus with his right foot, doubling him up like a concertina. Next, a short right uppercut slammed into Barry's face, opening his mouth up like a tin of jam and throwing him against the car. Blood bubbling down his chin, Barry tottered for a moment, then before Les could belt him again, he fell to his knees and pitched face-first onto the footpath, out cold. Wasting no time, Les walked straight across to the bloke with the hood up and slammed a left hook into his face, pulverising the bloke's nose. The unsuspecting bloke let out an agonised yelp, then went spinning back along the footpath, landing sprawled out over the taxi rank seat, holding his bloodied face.

Terrified at the monster they'd unexpectedly unleashed, the bloke in the brown jacket stepped back and pointed at Les. 'I'll get the cops onto you,' he whined. 'I'm gonna get the cops. You wait.'

'What?' Les reached over with his left hand and grabbed the bloke roughly by the collar. 'Four of you were going to get stuck into me and the girl. Now you want to run to the cops. You weak piece of shit.' Les swung his right hand back and bitch-slapped Brown Jacket across the face, splitting his lip. As he cried out with pain, Les gave him a crisp backhander, opening his mouth up some more, then bitch-slapped him again.

Keeping a wary distance, the remaining hero glared at Les. 'You're dead meat, arsehole,' he yelled. 'Dead. I'm gonna get me brothers. And we'll fuckin kill you.'

Les glared at him. 'You're going to get your brothers, are you? Well here, take your mate with you.' Les spun Brown Jacket around, gave him a push then booted him hard up the backside.

Holding his bleeding mouth, the bloke wobbled along the footpath and into his mate.

'Now piss off, the pair of you,' snapped Les, 'before you both get a blue suede shoe up your arse. Go on. Fuck off.' Les stared daggers at the two hoons for a moment then turned back, stepped past the bloke lying on the seat and around the unconscious Barry and took Marla by the arm. 'Come along, Marla,' he said calmly. 'Best we get out of here. This doesn't appear to be a very nice part of town.'

Still not quite sure what happened, Marla looked at the two men lying where Les had left them and the other two standing at the corner. 'Okay,' she said quietly.

They crossed the next corner and started up the hill before Les spoke. 'So did you have to get an AVO out against that dill's brother?' he asked.

'Milton? Yes. After I said I didn't want to see him any more, but we could still remain friends. He got . . . really angry.'

'Angry?'

'Yes. He tried to choke me, actually,' said Marla.

'Choke you? Ohh, what a hero,' sniggered Les.

'Don't worry,' said Marla. 'I nearly scratched his eyes out. So then he started stalking me. And threatening my friends. His family was the same. As you saw with Barry tonight. So I took out an AVO.'

'An AVO. Did it work?'

'Yes, sort of.'

'Sort of,' echoed Les. 'Marla, you can take out all the AVOs in the world, but nothing gets through to a mug better than a good smack in the mouth and a few broken bones. Bad luck your friend Milton wasn't here tonight.'

'Yes,' agreed Marla. 'But I'll tell you something, Les. Zac, the bloke you slapped across the face.'

'Yeah. What about him?'

'Well, he's got a brother and a cousin are cops in Gosford. And they're real turds. So you can bet he'll go running to them and try and have you up for assault.'

'Maybe,' said Les.

'And the last bloke, Hickey. He does come from a big family of nutters. And they will come looking for you. So be careful while you're in Terrigal.' Marla smiled up at Norton. 'I'd hate to see anything happen to you, Les. You're nice.'

Les took the Elvis sunglasses off and put them in his pocket. 'Why, thank you, ma'am,' he smiled back. 'Thank you very, very much.'

They proceeded on up to Ocean Star Apartments. Les opened the gate and Marla admired the fountain before they walked through the foyer. There was no one around. But the place was well lit and Marla noted all the paintings and furnishings before they took the lift to the first floor.

'Wow. These paintings just go on and on,' said Marla, as they followed the hallway down to Norton's apartment.

'Yes. They're nice, aren't they,' said Les. He put the key in the lock then pushed the door open. 'Anyway, Marla. Here's my room. It's a bit cramped. But if I move the fold-up bed, there's a bit more space.'

Les had left the loungeroom light on. He flicked the light on in the hallway as Marla stepped inside then closed the door behind them. Marla walked down to the loungeroom then turned around and gaped at Les.

'This is your room?' she said.

'That's right,' nodded Les. 'Like I said. It's reasonable.'

'Reasonable? Reasonable? It's ... it's out of this world.'

'What?' shrugged Les. 'Doesn't everybody stay in a place like this when they're on holidays?'

Marla took in the surroundings. 'Those paintings,' she pointed. 'They're bloody Brett Whiteleys. This glass table. It's inlaid with pure onyx. The chandeliers are all crystal.'

'They light the place up, I suppose,' said Les. 'Come and have a look at this.' He opened the sliding glass door and led Marla out onto the balcony. The moon was shimmering on the glassy water in the Haven and the ships were still necklaced across the horizon. In the far distance Norah Head lighthouse was flashing its friendly beam out over the ocean.

'Not a bad view.'

'Not a bad view?' Marla's voice tailed off then she stepped over and stood directly in front of Norton. 'Les. What are you? Some kind of weird, millionaire eccentric?'

Les shook his head. 'No. Just a battling widower taking a brief holiday on the beautiful Central Coast. That's all.'

'Yeah, that'd be right.' Marla pulled Les towards her and wrapped her arms his neck. 'Come here, you big goose,' she said, then kissed him flush on the lips.

Half full of bourbon and in an extra good mood, there wasn't much Les could do, except kiss Marla back. The kiss went on a bit, and on a bit more. Marla slipped the tongue in and Norton's big hands started wandering all over her whippy body. Finally they came up for air and opened their eyes.

'I'll tell you what, Marla,' said Les. 'I got an idea. How would you like a swim, and wash all that smoke and crap out of your hair?'

'A swim?' Marla gave a little shiver. 'It's a bit Piccadilly, isn't it?'

Les shook his head. 'There's a heated indoor pool downstairs. And I got two huge fluffy bathrobes in my room. I can make us a delicious each and we can take them with us.'

Marla looked at Les for a moment. 'Okay,' she said. 'Will the pool still be open?'

'It's all right,' replied Les. 'I've got a key.'

Les took Marla into his bedroom and got two dark blue bathrobes out of the closet and placed them on the bed. While she was getting changed, Les went to the kitchen, found two highball glasses and filled them with ice, bourbon and soda water. He placed them on the granite kitchen bar table just as Marla walked barefooted into the kitchen wearing her robe and a towel over her shoulder.

'These are so comfy,' she said, tugging her robe. 'They're unreal.'

'Good.' Les pointed to the glasses. 'There's your drink,' he said. 'I'll be back in a sec.'

Les went to the bedroom and stripped off. His Speedos had dried hanging on the back of the chair, so he slipped them on. As he did, Les noticed Mr Wobbly was starting to get a little interested in what was going on, so Les gave him a gentle pat on the head.

'Now you just behave yourself, okay?' said Les. 'And don't go embarrassing me in front of anyone.'

Les slipped into his robe, put the zinger in one pocket and the key in the other, got a towel and walked out to the kitchen.

'Hey. You don't make a bad drink,' said Marla, holding up her glass.

Les picked his glass up and took a sip. 'Shit,' he said. 'Jack sure lives round here, don't he.'

'Just nice,' said Marla. 'Hey. Who were you talking to in there?' she asked.

'No one,' replied Les. 'I was just singing. Come on. Let's go twisting by the pool.'

'Sounds good to me.'

Holding their drinks, they took the lift down to the lobby then walked across to the pool and the gymnasium. The lights were on, but the main door was locked. Les slipped the zinger in the lock and had it open in seconds. The door to the pool was also locked. The zinger hummed and it was open quicker than the first one. After the cool night air, it felt like a sauna when they stepped inside.

'Wow. How good's this?' said Marla, looking up at all the lights twinkling like tiny stars in the ceiling. Suddenly she peered across the pool at the Egyptian motifs and hieroglyphics and put her hand over her mouth. 'Oh my God,' she exclaimed. 'This is totally bizarre.'

'Bizarre,' said Les. 'What do you mean, bizarre?'

'It's too much of a coincidence,' said Marla, staring at the opposite wall.

'Coincidence? What are you talking about?'

'I'll tell you later.' Marla stared at the wall a moment longer, then shook her head and started to loosen her robe. 'I don't believe it,' she muttered. 'I simply don't believe it.'

'Whatever,' shrugged Les.

He took his robe off and placed it on one of the wicker chairs, along with his towel and drink, then stood there in his Speedos. When he turned around, Marla had taken her robe off as well and was standing next to one of the chairs wearing a pair of lacy blue knickers. And she had a red hot body.

'Come on,' laughed Marla. 'Last one in's a poofter.'

'Keep that up, you bitch,' said Les, 'and you'll feel the weight of my handbag.'

Together they plunged into the pool and pushed across to the other side. The water felt wonderful, lovely and warm and crystal clear.

'Ohh how good's this,' said Marla, tossing her head back when they surfaced. 'I feel like I'm born again. What a good idea.'

'Yeah. It's not bad, is it,' agreed Les.

They swam and frolicked around, splashed a bit of water at each other and did all the stupid things people do when they're drunk and having a good time. Eventually the frolicking settled down and they swam up to each other, then drifted in front of the chairs and tables. Marla's eyes were sparkling and her hair was shining in the soft light coming from the tiny stars in the ceiling; after watching Marla's tight backside going up and down in the water and her boobs sitting on top of it, Norton's eyes were sparkling as well. Besides that, Mr Wobbly had totally ignored what Les told him earlier and he was poking up under Norton's Speedos demanding in on the action. Marla floated over to Les and put her arms around his neck.

'Oohh Les,' she purred. 'Is that a snorkel in your Speedos? Or are you just glad to see me?'

'Marla. I can't lie,' grinned Les. 'I'm horribly, diabolically, monstrously glad to see you.'

Les ran his hands up over Marla's ribs then kissed her. Marla kissed him back, slipped her sweet tongue in and after that there was a lot of disturbance in the water. Les groped Marla and kissed her lovely boobs, Marla groped Les, put a stranglehold on him and shoved her tongue in his ear. Les did the same and ran his hand between Marla's legs, feeling the sleek softness of her pubic hair beneath the water. Marla ducked her head under the water and gave Les a quick underwater polish that sent Les into orbit.

By now both Les and Mr Wobbly had had enough. Les helped Marla out of the pool, slid her knickers off, along with his Speedos, then lay his bathrobe down next to the chairs and tables and lowered Marla onto it. He knelt down in front of her and Marla spread her legs. Les took Marla under the shoulders, kissed her tenderly, then eased himself inside.

Marla gasped and the first few strokes made Norton's eyes spin. He gathered momentum, Marla invited him in and Les went for it. It was fabulous and with Marla spread out rock solid on the floor with nowhere to go, Les was able to give her everything. He kept going as long as he could. But full of bourbon and feeling the warmth and loveliness of Marla's body, it was too good. Marla squealed and grabbed hold of Les. Les stiffened his legs, pushed with all his might, then groaned while Marla squealed as he emptied out. Finally they settled down and had a drink, then Les stood and took hold of Marla's hand.

'Come on, Marla,' he said quietly. 'I got a great idea.'

Les placed the bathrobe at the side of the pool then took Marla back into the water and swam her around a little before taking her back down to the shallow end where he'd placed the bathrobe. He lifted Marla out of the pool, placed her backside on the bathrobe, then opened her legs and, standing against the edge of the pool, gave Marla a gigantic eat.

Marla couldn't believe it. She thrashed around on the bathrobe and grabbed Les by the hair, kicked her legs up in the air like a bucking bronco and cried with delight. Les kept going till Marla let go a long, low moan and emptied out in Norton's face. Les smiled and continued eating a little longer, savouring his impromptu meal, like he was in a Michelin four-star café in France, dining on truffle sauce.

By now it was getting late and Les and Marla were both gone. They had a last swim and a kiss and a cuddle, then finished their drinks, put their robes on and went back to Norton's apartment.

Les filled two glasses with cold water and they drank them while they got changed; Marla into what she'd been wearing, Les into a pair of shorts and a plain white T-shirt. He put the stereo on and found a little soft FM music, then sat on the lounge with his arm around Marla.

'Marla,' Les said, sincerely. 'This has been one of the best nights I've ever had. Truly. Meeting you was the last thing I was expecting.'

'Les,' smiled Marla, giving him a soft kiss on the lips. 'You took the words right out of my mouth.'

'Thanks, Marla.'

Marla looked quizzically at Norton as the music played in the background. 'Les,' she asked. 'What are you doing tomorrow?'

'Nothing much,' shrugged Les. 'Go for a swim. Hang around. Get your phone number before you leave, so I can ring you up and annoy the shit out of you.'

'How would you like me to show you something you've never seen before in your life? And you can do me a favour at the same time.'

'Sounds intriguing,' queried Les. 'What is it?'

'I'll tell you tomorrow. I'll call around in the morning. Not too early,' Marla smiled. 'And we'll go in my car. It's not that far from here.'

'Okay,' said Les. 'I'm not easy to get. But you've got me.'

'Good.' Marla looked at her watch. 'Now I'd better get home. Mum and Dad don't like me staying out all night.'

'Fair enough. I'll ring you a taxi. What's the number?'

'I'll do it.' Marla used the phone in the kitchen then came back into the loungeroom. 'The woman said one would be here in five minutes.'

'Okey doke.'

Les walked down to the security gate and exchanged mobile phone numbers with Marla while they waited for the taxi. He told her just to ask for Les in apartment eight when she arrived in the morning, the manager would let her in and she could come straight up. They had time for a kiss and a bit of small talk then the taxi arrived. Les opened the back door and gave Marla two twenties.

'Les. I only live at Wamberal,' she told him.

'Marla,' smiled Les. 'You're forgetting. I'm some sort of weird, eccentric millionaire. I'll see you tomorrow.' Les closed the door and blew Marla a kiss. The last thing he saw was the cab disappearing down the hill and Marla waving out the back window. Les yawned, shivered in the cool night air for a moment as he took in the stars, then went back to the apartment.

Les had another drink of water, cleaned his teeth then switched off the stereo and the lights and fell into bed. He yawned once, smiled, then pushed his head into the pillows and went out like a light. It had been a big night.

Les blinked his eyes open the next morning and momentarily peered round the sunlit room wondering where he was before everything came together. He smiled contentedly, yawned, then checked his watch, got out of bed and padded across to the bedroom window. Outside, it looked like another beautiful day in Terrigal: the sun was beaming down from an azure sky while a light, off-shore breeze gently ruffled the water and quietly rocked the boats in the Haven. Les stretched, took a few deep breaths, then walked across to the ensuite. When he'd finished, he changed into a dry pair of Speedos and gave his white, Jimmy Buffett T-shirt another run over a pair of dark blue cargoes, then went to the kitchen, got a glass of water and took it out onto the balcony to admire the view.

It didn't take long before Les figured the view would look better from behind a pair of sunglasses and his head would feel better after a couple of painkillers. He dropped two Panadeine, put his sunnies on and went back out on the balcony. The sunglasses definitely helped and the water felt good going down. But food, and plenty of it, would go down even better. Les decided to walk down to Terrigal, take a dip in the ocean, get the paper and have breakfast at Serene's again. By the time he got back, Marla should be around to whisk him away to wherever the mysterious place was she intended whisking him away to. Les threw a towel in his bag, got some money and took the lift to the foyer.

Besides a cleaner and a gardener, there were a few people strolling around. One or two gave Norton's bruised face a second look. Les smiled back at them before putting his sunglasses on then continuing on out the gate and down the hill.

The tide was up and the water felt sensational when Les dived in. He wallowed around, loosened up the cobwebs and lay on his back spurting water up in the air. Ahh yes, this is the life, he grinned. A few more days up here and I won't know myself. Les flopped around a while longer, then got out, dried off and put his clothes back on before walking down to the paper shop, where he got another friendly smile from the woman in glasses.

Les found the same seat as the day before at Serene's. He didn't expect to find Carol and got the tall woman with the glasses. Unlike Carol, she was all smiles and politeness. Les had a double shot latte to get the ball rolling and ordered the same meal as yesterday, plus a blueberry muffin. Everything arrived promptly, Les ordered another latte and ripped in.

Breakfast seemed to taste even better than the day before and the blueberry muffin was to die for. Steam rose in the air when Les tore it open to add butter and it was packed with sweet, fat blueberries. Les was glad no one in the restaurant knew him, because he was stuffing food down his throat like a steam shovel. Les finished the paper over his second coffee, paid the bill, left the smiling woman in glasses a tip, and walked back to the resort. Glen was behind the desk when Les walked in. Les gave him a wave as he headed for the lift.

'Oh Les. Have you got a minute?' Glen asked.

'Sure,' replied Les, walking back to the desk. 'What's up?'

'You didn't get into any trouble, down Terrigal last night, did you Les?' enquired Glen.

'Trouble? I got pretty drunk, I know that,' answered Les. 'Why?'

'A cop from Gosford rang me earlier. Some men got assaulted with a baseball bat near the beer garden late last night. They didn't get a good description,' chuckled Glen, 'because the bloke was wearing Elvis Presley sunglasses of all things. But they said he was a fairly big bloke, with a square jaw and reddish brown hair. That wouldn't be you, surely Les?'

Les grimaced and shook his head. 'Glen. I can assure you, I don't go around bashing people with baseball bats. I never have. And especially not when I'm on holidays.'

'No. I didn't think so,' said Glen. 'Anyway. The cops said they might come round later and check the place out. They think the bloke might be staying here or live round this way somewhere.'

'Fair enough,' said Les. 'I won't be far away. Oh Glen,' he added. 'A girl will be calling round for me this morning. Her name's Marla. Will you let her in?'

'Sure Les. Not a problem.'

'Thanks mate.' The phone rang, Les left the manager to it and continued across to the lift.

Back in the apartment, Les stepped out onto the balcony, stared at the ocean and shook his head. Can you believe it? Those four pricks started everything, and as soon as a couple got sat on their arse, they went crying to the police. And they said I used a baseball bat. Fair dinkum. A big, fat pelican zoomed in over the water like a flying boat, landed on its big, fat feet, and joined a few of its friends paddling around in front of some fishermen cleaning their catch by the boat ramp. I only hope it doesn't put a dampener on my holiday, Les scowled. It's just starting to get good. Les went inside, switched on the stereo and tidied up his room. He was making the bed when there was a soft knock on the door. One thing for sure, smiled Les, fluffing the last pillow, that's definitely not the wallopers. He walked down the hall and opened the door. Marla was standing there wearing a white T-shirt tucked into a pair of jeans, a khaki photographer's vest, gym boots and a white baseball cap.

'Yes, young lady?' asked Les. 'How can I help you?'

'Well, you could start by giving me a hug,' replied Marla.

'That shouldn't be too much of a problem,' smiled Les. He put his arms around Marla and gave her a cuddle and a little kiss. 'How are you this morning?' he asked her.

'Seedy. But all right. Can I have a glass of water?'

'Sure. Come in.' Les ushered Marla into the kitchen and poured her a glass of cold water. 'So what's happening?' he asked her, after she had a few good swallows.

'Well, I hate to tell you this, Les,' said Marla. 'But the police were round my place this morning.'

'You too,' replied Les. He told Marla what Glen told him down at the desk. 'So what did they say to you?'

Marla shook her head. 'Nothing. I was still in bed and Mum told them I wasn't home. But they said they'd call round again.'

'Terrific,' said Les.

'Not only that. Hickey rang me up and abused me. Milton was

with him. And Hickey said he and his brothers are going to get you. And he's bringing some mates as well.'

'They got to find me first,' shrugged Les.

'They'll find you, Les,' said Marla. 'Terrigal isn't Sydney.'

'Yeah. Fair enough. But Jesus,' protested Les, 'I don't know what they're all blowing up about. It's not as if anyone got hurt that much.'

'Not as if anyone got hurt that much,' echoed Marla. 'Barry's in hospital with a ruptured sternum, fifteen stitches in his mouth, and a depressed fracture of the skull.'

'He fell over and hit his head,' said Les. 'You saw that yourself.'

Marla ignored Les. 'Andrew's got a broken nose and a fractured cheekbone. And Zac, the one you just slapped. Well, I suppose he's not so bad. He's only got eight stitches in his mouth and a limp.'

'There you go,' smiled Les. 'It's not all doom and gloom.'

'Christ, Les,' said Marla. 'For a widowed motel owner, you're a steppin' razor dog. You're walkin' talkin' bad news.'

'Well, I'm not always like that.' Les suddenly snapped his fingers. 'You know what it was, Marla. Those Elvis Presley sunglasses.'

'The sunglasses? What the hell did they have to do with it?'

'They had a spell on them.'

'A spell?' Marla screwed her face up. 'What are you talking about?'

'Like that movie *The Mask*,' explained Les. 'When Jim Carrey put the mask on, he turned into a crazy person. The same thing happened to me when I put those sunglasses on. I was possessed by an evil power.' Les pointed directly at Marla. 'One thing for sure, Marla. We must get rid of them before they cause any more damage.'

Marla finished her water and placed the glass down. 'You know, Les,' she said. 'I think that's what attracted me to you. You're quite mad.'

'Well,' answered Les, 'at least I know it. There's a lot of people out there are mad and don't know it. And that's not good.'

'Yes. I suppose you're right,' Marla agreed.

'Of course I'm right. Now,' smiled Les, 'let's put all this foolishment behind us, and tell me what's going on. Where are you taking me?'

Marla sat down on a bar stool in the kitchen. 'I'm taking you to a cave,' she said.

'A cave. Ooh, I don't know about caves, Marla,' shivered Les. 'They're all dark and horrible. And full of spiders and snakes and other creepy crawlies.'

Marla shook her head. 'This one's all right. And I want you to video me while I'm in there. My video's automatic focus. All you have to do is aim and shoot.'

'I think I can handle that,' said Les.

'I want to get out there ASAP, because the National Parks and Wildlife are about to block off the access road. And you'll only be able to get in there by foot or mountain bike. And it's five kilometres.'

'Okay. So what's in this cave?' asked Les. 'Lost treasures? Are we going to play *Raiders of the Lost Ark*? I bags being Indiana Jones.'

Marla shook her head. 'Nothing like that. But have you got a camera?'

'I sure have.'

'Well, bring it, and you'll get some good photos. But just promise me you won't tell too many people about what you've seen. It would be awful if someone got in there and vandalised it.'

'No. You can trust me,' Les assured her.

'Good.' Marla got up from her stool. 'Okay, handsome. Let's go.'

'All right. Just give my hair time to dry while I finish watching *Days of Our Lives*.'

Les went to his room and threw a couple of things in his bag. He got a bottle of water from the kitchen, then he and Marla took the lift down to the lobby. Parked out front was a maroon Ford Laser in good condition with a backpack on the rear seat. Les sat in the front and placed his bag on the floor, Marla got behind the wheel and with the car stereo quietly playing local FM they proceeded out the gate and turned right up Scenic Highway. Les and Marla didn't say a lot as they drove along. Marla appeared to be concentrating on something and Les was thinking about his situation between the local wallopers and the local hoons. They passed Erina Plaza, then Bluetongue Stadium further along, and were heading towards West Gosford when Marla turned to Les.

'Have you thought over what you're going to do about the police and Milton and his mates?' she asked him.

'Yes I have,' answered Les.

'And . . .?'

'I'm going to get stuck into the bastards again,' he declared. 'The cops too.'

'You're what?' said Marla.

Les reached into his bag and took out the Elvis sunglasses. He put them on and grinned at Marla. 'Somebody — stop me.'

'Jesus, Les,' said Marla. 'Take them off. If the police see you . . .'

'Smmmokkkinnnn.'

Marla shook her head. 'You are mad. Totally.'

'You're right, Marla,' said Les, removing the sunglasses and placing them back in his bag. 'I could feel their evil powers as soon as I put them on. It's wrong. I want to use my secret powers for good, Marla.'

'Yes. You do that, Les,' she answered.

They passed the turn-off to Woy Woy and started up a steep, curving road into the mountains. Les wasn't sure exactly where he was, but he knew they were heading out of Gosford towards the F3 and Sydney. His window was down and outside he could hear the ringing of bellbirds echoing through the trees and gullies.

'Hey, listen to those bellbirds, Marla,' said Les. 'Don't they sound fabulous.'

'Yes. You're in Henry Kendall country now, Les,' she replied.

Marla followed the traffic to the top of the mountain before taking a turn-off. Houses went by and soon it was nothing but trees and scrub on either side of the road. Marla appeared to be looking for something before she slowed down at a barely perceptible opening amongst the trees.

'Here it is,' she said.

Marla swung the Laser off the road and they began following a rough, narrow trail surrounded by boulders, rugged bush and overhanging trees. The further they went, the worse the trail got, until it was nothing more than two wheel marks worn into the mud and rocks. Just past a huge grey log they came to a fork. Marla went left and they continued to bump along till she came to another fork and veered left again. After another kilometre of bone-rattling trail, they entered a sloping clearing that finished at a line of scrubby trees and bush. Behind the clearing was a long granite cliff, high enough to cast a shadow over the clearing. Its rugged face was dotted with spinifex and cycads, while red gums and eucalyptus trees grew in wild profusion along the top. Marla drove to the edge of the clearing and switched off the engine.

'Here we are,' she said. 'The cave's up in that ridge.'

'Up there?' said Les, peering out the windscreen. 'Shit!'

Norton peered out the windscreen a moment or two longer, then picked up his bag and got out of the car. Marla was standing by the door, climbing into her backpack.

'Which way now?' Les asked her, putting his backpack on.

Marla adjusted her cap and gave her shoulders a shrug. 'Follow me.'

'You're the boss.'

There was no path. Marla knew where she was going and Les fell in behind. The bush rose up, then they came to the cliff face. Marla found a narrow trail going left along a ridge and Les followed her as the trail doubled back on itself and went right. As they climbed along the ridge, Les could see the distant ocean through the valleys. But no sign of civilisation; apart from the birds and a light westerly eerily flicking through the trees, it was almost silent. Les followed Marla along the second trail before she stopped at a narrow opening in the granite on their left. It was barely head high and the way the trail angled on, if you didn't know the opening was there you would quite easily miss it.

'Righto, Les,' smiled Marla. 'See if you're ready for this.'

Les followed Marla through the opening and stopped dead in his tracks. It wasn't really a cave, but two granite walls, fifteen metres long and ten metres high, leaning slightly towards each other. They were open at the top and separated by a floor of rock and soil two metres wide, with another opening at the opposite end. The walls were spread with lichen and beneath the lichen, countless Egyptian hieroglyphs had been carved into the flinty granite.

'Holy bloody shit!' said Les. 'Who did all this?'

'I don't know,' smiled Marla. 'You tell me.'

There were scarab beetles, mummies, five pointed stars, radiating suns and birds. Sphinxes, water signs, drinking vessels, hands, eyes, snakes, curved rods, boats, angled lines and circles. Anything you would find painted inside an ancient Egyptian temple was carved into the two facing walls of the cave. Some carvings were inside cartouches. They went as high as ten metres and as low as a metre from the floor. There wasn't a chip on the wall or a mistake, every carving had been executed in perfect detail. The wall on the right split into a fissure and the hieroglyphs continued on the other side, where carved down on the left was Thoth, the scribe of the Gods. There was no mistaking the figure of a man with the head of an ibis, dressed in priestly robes, holding a lamp, ready to convey souls to a place of higher learning.

Les turned to Marla, gobsmacked. 'I've never seen anything like this in my life. Especially not out in the middle of the Australian bush.'

'Now you know why I got a bit excited in the pool last night,' said Marla.

'But who did it?' asked Les, staring around the cave.

'I don't know. I rang two professors of Egyptology in Sydney. And they got all uptight and tried to tell me some diggers did it when they came back from the First World War.'

'What?' said Les. 'The average digger in the First World War was a country boy about seventeen years old. Half of them couldn't read or write properly, let alone have the skill to carve something like this.'

'My thoughts exactly,' smiled Marla. 'And why would they do it anyway? And why out here?'

'Yeah. There'd be bugger all round here just after the First World War,' agreed Les.

'Now take a look at this.' Marla pointed out a carving level with her face, a little away from the others. It was an oblong, half a metre in length with little circles along the side, standing on four legs. 'What's that look like, Les?' she asked.

Les stared at the carving. 'Well, it ain't a beetle, that's for sure.' He turned to Marla. 'A spaceship?'

'That's what I reckon,' answered Marla. 'And did the diggers, or anybody else for that matter, know anything about UFOs back in nineteen eighteen?'

'I doubt it,' said Les.

'Now come and have a look at this.'

Marla led Les to the other end of the cave and they climbed over a pile of rocks at the opening. Just to the right, three thick boards, a metre or so long, were sitting on the ground with a large rock on top of them.

'Give me a hand to move these boards, Les,' said Marla. 'The National Parks put them there so people wouldn't fall down.'

'Righto,' said Les.

Les moved the rock first, then they both moved the boards to reveal a two-metre deep pit, edged with jutting boulders. At the bottom was a perfectly straight, stone ledge with a narrow gap beneath it.

'What's that down there?' asked Les. 'It looks like a ledge.'

'It is,' said Marla. 'I haven't been under it, because the gap's too narrow. But I'm told it's a big square room carved out of solid rock.'

'You're kidding?' Les stared down into the pit in disbelief, then turned to Marla. 'So how did you get onto all this?' he asked her.

'I've got a girlfriend works for Gosford Council,' replied Marla. 'She brought me out here. And I came out a couple of times on my own. Then I decided to video it and offer the story to one of the TV networks. I got a few contacts between Newcastle and Sydney.'

'Won't all that publicity expose everything?' said Les.

Marla shook her head. 'There's already been photos and a story about the cave published in a New Age magazine. And I'll keep the location secret. No one will know where it is.'

'Fair enough,' nodded Les. 'If you didn't know the exact spot, you wouldn't find it in a hundred years.'

'Exactly,' said Marla. 'So let's put these boards back and you can start filming.'

They replaced the boards and the rock, then dropped their backpacks on the floor of the cave. While Marla was sorting out her video camera, Les got his camera and started taking photos. He got Marla to take some of him with the hieroglyphics in the background and he took some of Marla. Finally, Marla had everything together and Les had her camcorder in his hands, ready to go.

'Start with me standing in the middle of the cave,' said Marla. 'Then follow me around while I point things out.'

'Okay,' said Les. 'If there's any hiccups, we can just rewind and shoot again.'

'Exactly.' Marla stepped into the the middle of the cave. 'Okay,' she said. 'Let's do it.'

Les squared her up in the side viewer and pressed record. 'Righto,' he said quietly. 'Roll film. Roll sound. Annnnddd — action.'

'Hello,' smiled Marla. 'I'm Marla Ritchie. And I'm standing in a cave near the Hawkesbury River in New South Wales, where I'm about to show you something you may not believe. But trust me. It's all true.'

Les followed Marla around with the camcorder like a pro, zeroing in on the particular carvings she'd point out, taking close-ups of her and panning round the walls while she spoke. At the same time, Marla was a natural. She spoke slowly and clearly, moved well and rarely fluffed a line. They checked the film every now and again and both agreed, you couldn't tell the difference between their efforts and what you saw on *Sixty Minutes*. They took a shot of the boards but didn't bother to move them, got a shot of the open ceiling and one of a lizard hiding in the fissure. At the end, Marla stood next to the carving of the spaceship and smiled enigmatically into the camera.

'This is Marla Ritchie, somewhere near the Hawkesbury River. Thank you for your time.'

'Annnnd — cut,' said Les. 'Okay. That's a wrap. Check the gate and let's have lunch. Principals first. Extras can wait.'

'You've done this before, Les,' smiled Marla.

'I did a TV commercial once,' said Les. 'A beer one.'

'Yeah? What was that like?'

'It ended up in a gigantic brawl.'

Maria looked at her watch. 'Shit! I'm going to have to make a move. Dad's away. And I promised Mum I'd run her down to the dentist.'

'No worries,' said Les.

Marla stepped over and put her arms around Les. 'Hey, thanks for doing this, Les. I really appreciate it.'

'You don't have to thank me, Marla,' replied Les. 'Thank you for bringing me out here. It's one of the most fantastic things I've ever seen.'

'My pleasure,' smiled Maria. She gave Les a quick kiss then let him go. 'But before we leave, Les. About the diggers coming back from the war and carving all this.' Marla pointed to the walls. 'You see all the lichen growing everywhere. You know how old that gets, don't you?'

Les ran his fingers across a patch of lichen growing over an ibis carved into the wall. 'Yeah. Real old,' he answered.

'Well, my friend at Gosford Council said a piece of lichen from here had been carbon dated. It was two hundred years old. And it was growing over one of the carvings. So I'd say that shoots the diggers theory down in flames.'

'Shit! Does it what,' replied Les.

Marla had a drink of water then placed her camcorder in her backpack. 'Come on,' she said. 'Let's get going.'

'Righto.' Les threw his bag over his shoulder and followed Marla out of the cave.

Not a lot was said on the journey back to Terrigal. Apart from being blown out by what he'd seen in the cave, Les was running a number of things over in his head. Marla was no doubt concentrating on how she was going to frame what they'd just filmed before she offered it to the TV networks. Before Les knew it they'd passed the hotel coming into Terrigal and were slowing down for the speed humps in front of the shops along the beachfront.

'Bad luck we haven't got time for a bit of lunch,' said Les, as they drove past Serene's.

'Yes. All that exploring and filming's made me rather peckish,' smiled Marla.

Les returned her smile. 'Maybe some other time, Marla?'

'I'll keep you to that, Les.'

They approached Ocean Star Apartments and Marla was about to cross the double lines and swing into the driveway when a white Holden driven by a bull-necked man in a grey suit with another bull-necked man in a suit, sitting alongside him, swung out of the driveway and continued on up the Scenic Highway.

'Shit!' said Marla jumping on the brakes. 'You know who that was, don't you?'

'No,' replied Les. 'But allowing for my timing, and going by their big boofheads, I've got a pretty good idea.'

Marla checked for other cars then swung the maroon Laser up into the driveway. She cut the engine and turned to Les with a concerned look on her face.

'Seriously, Les,' asked Marla, 'what are you going to do about last night?'

'What am I doing?' answered Les. 'I'm going back to Sydney.'

Marla placed her hand on Norton's leg. 'Les,' she said. 'I think that's the best thing to do.'

'Yeah,' sniffed Les. 'You're only saying that because you want to get rid of me.'

'No. No way.' Marla was adamant. 'I like you, Les. A lot. Your washing machine's definitely not going the full cycle. But no man's ever made me laugh as much as you have.' Marla lowered her eyes. 'Or seduced me so sweetly. I want to see you again.'

Norton couldn't help but feel warm inside. 'And I want to see you again too, Marla,' he said. 'Come here.' Les placed his hand on Marla's cheek, tenderly drew her face towards him and kissed her long and soft. He let Marla go then smiled into her eyes. 'Go on. You better go and get your mum.'

'Make sure you ring me,' said Marla.

'I will,' replied Les. He picked up his bag, opened the car door and got out.

'Goodbye, Les. Be careful driving home,' said Marla.

'No worries.' Les closed the door, Marla backed out of the driveway and bipped the horn then drove off towards the beachfront. Les smiled and waved goodbye before his expression abruptly changed. 'Fuck it!' he cursed, and walked into the resort.

Glen was behind the desk when Les entered the reception area and by the look on his face, Les could clearly see there was something on the manager's mind. Before he could say anything, Les decided to get in first.

'Hey Glen,' smiled Les. 'How are you?'

'Oh, I'm good, Les,' hesitated the manager. 'How are you?'

'Up to shit,' replied Les.

'Oh. Why's that?'

'I just got a call from Eddie. There's been a bit of trouble at the club and I have to get back to Sydney. Pronto.'

The manager rolled his eyes as a look of pure relief swept over his dapper face. Les had no doubt he'd been trying to do the right thing by Eddie and keep the local police on side at the same time.

'Gee, that's no good, Les,' said Glen.

'Tell me about it,' grunted Les. 'Anyway. I'll go up and get my gear. I'll be back very shortly.'

'Okay, Les.'

Norton walked down the hall and caught the lift to his apartment. He dropped his backpack in the bedroom then went to the kitchen, got the last of the mineral water from the fridge and took it onto the sundeck to check out the view for the last time. With the sun sparkling on the ocean, it looked more beautiful than ever.

'Thanks, mate,' said Les, looking up at the sky. 'You couldn't help yourself. Could you?'

Les finished the mineral water, went inside and packed his gear. It didn't take long. When he was satisfied he had everything, Les locked the apartment and caught the lift down to the lobby.

'Shit. That was quick,' said Glen, as Les approached the desk.

'Mate,' replied Les, 'when Price says get your finger out, he means get your finger out.'

'Nothing too serious, I hope,' said Glen.

'Well, between you and me,' said Les, sliding the keys across the desk. 'There was a double murder in the club. Two members of an Asian Triad.'

'Bloody hell!' exclaimed Glen.

'But don't worry, Glen,' winked Les. 'You won't read anything about it in the papers.'

'Yes,' Glen nodded. 'I know how you boys operate.'

'Not exactly by the rules,' smiled Les. 'But apart from that, Glen, this place is absolutely fantastic. Okay if I stay here again?'

'Hey, Les,' gestured Glen, 'any time, mate. Just give me a couple of days' notice.'

'Unreal,' beamed Les. 'Well, I'd better get going. Thanks again, Glen.'

'Les,' smiled the manager, 'it was a pleasure having you here.'

Les walked down to the garage, threw his gear in the Berlina and left the resort. After a quick lap of Terrigal he reluctantly nosed the Berlina towards The Entrance Road and the F3.

While the shops at Erina were going past, Les rehashed what he'd been thinking about earlier in the car with Marla. It burnt his arse something awful having to end his holiday because of a few would-be tough guys. But it wouldn't be much fun if a whole team of idiots jumped him one night or whenever. And you could bet they'd be the ones with the baseball bats. Then there was the local wallopers. They'd have no trouble nailing him on an assault charge. It was his word and Marla's against four others. Plus, with all his form, they'd oppose bail. And a cell in Gosford wouldn't be anywhere near as nice as his apartment at Ocean Star Resort.

Les was also spooked about Rose the tarot card reader's uncanny predictions. She said he'd find someone from the past. And he bumped into Houston. He'd find something really old. And Marla took him to a cave full of Egyptian hieroglyphs. And along two trails. She also told him to expect the unexpected. The last thing he expected was to get into a fight, and for the pricks that started it to go running to the police and turn his quiet holiday on its head. So all up, he was better off getting out of town while he was still in front. Which wasn't the end of the world. Everything would eventually blow over and he could come back, stay at the resort again and catch up with Marla. Thinking of Marla made Les smile. What would she say when the widowed millionaire motel owner turned up at her door, driving a battered Berlina with a rotten smell coming from the back? Before Les knew it, he'd climbed out of Kariong and was at the F3. He slipped on a tape and with Adam Harvey twanging out 'Genie in the Bottle', helped of course by Rod McCormack, Les put his foot down and headed for Bondi and home.

The traffic going back to Sydney was awful. A caravan flipped on the southern side of the Moonee Moonee Bridge, a car caught fire a kilometre back from the Hawkesbury River, a bus caused a pile-up at Killara and to top things off, a truck broke down on an approach to the Harbour Tunnel. When Les pulled up outside Chez Norton, it felt like midnight and his happy hat had vanished, he was starving hungry and bursting for a leak. He stormed in the front door, threw his bag in the bedroom and strode to the bathroom. When he finished, Les stared at the miserable face looking back at him in the mirror.

'Welcome home, Shithead,' he grunted.

Les went to the kitchen, almost ripped the door off the fridge then snarled his way through two bananas and a glass of

Ovaltine. He was that filthy he wouldn't talk to himself. He didn't even want his shadow hanging around. Norton didn't get like this too often. But when he did, he knew there was only one thing to do. Go somewhere 'away from the madding crowd' and run it out. Les changed into his training gear and drove down to Centennial Park. After parking at the bottom of Birrell Street, he did a few stretches, wrapped an old sweat rag round his head and took off. Going nowhere in particular. Just burning up an hour, jogging around the duck ponds and bush trails till he got over an extreme case of shit on the liver.

It was dark when Les returned home. He walked straight into the kitchen, took a large bottle of mineral water out of the fridge and started drinking. Although his heart rate was still up, his feet were sore and he stank of BO. Norton felt much better. While he was gulping down water, he checked the answering machine. There were no messages and something else dawned on him: the whole time he was away, he never turned his mobile phone on. Les got it from his bag, clicked it on and left it on the kitchen table, then threw his smelly gear in the laundry and got under the shower.

When he got out, Norton's condition continued to improve. He had to dodge around a few cuts and bruises when he was shaving. But looking at the face wincing back at him in the mirror as he gingerly dabbed a little bay rum on it, Les was convinced he'd returned to his shiny, happy, loveable, laughable self. He changed into a clean white T-shirt and a dark blue tracksuit, then went back to the kitchen and took an icy cold long neck from the fridge. Norton was enjoying it and wondering how much food would be enough for dinner when his mobile rang.

'Hello?'

'Hello, my friend.'

Les recognised the raspy voice. 'Deep Throat.'

'That is right,' replied the voice. 'So where have you been, my friend? I have been trying to ring you.'

'Where have I been? Nowhere. I forgot to turn my phone on. That's all,' Les lied.

'I see,' answered the voice. 'So what happened on Sunday? Did you go to that address I told you?'

'Yeah. Yeah I did,' replied Les.

'And what happened?'

'What happened? Nothing,' said Les. 'I had a good look around. But I'm buggered if I could see any bag. Are you sure that was the right address?'

'Oh yes,' said the voice. 'One hundred per cent.'

'Well, there was nothing there,' said Les. 'A bit of a mess maybe. But that was all.'

'I see. Ahhh . . .' Suddenly the voice sneezed violently.

'Gesundheit,' said Les.

'Yeah. Something like that,' sniffled the voice. 'All right,' the voice continued. 'I have another address for you.'

'You have?' For a moment Les was going to tell Deep Throat what he could do with his latest address. But Rose the tarot card reader told him he needed guidance and she'd been spot-on so far. 'All right. Where is it this time?'

'Still in Bondi,' said the voice. 'In Lamrock Avenue. Near Chambers Avenue. It is a semi cottage.'

'A semi. So how do I get in?' asked Les.

'That is up to you, my friend. But two women live there. Both are notorious thieves. They have the green bag with the eagle on the side.'

'Are you sure this time?' asked Les.

'Yes. One hundred per cent,' said the voice. 'If you go there in the afternoon, there should not be anybody home.'

Les thought about his zinger. This would be a snack. 'Okay,' he said.

'Do you have a Biro?' the voice continued.

'Yeah. Right here.'

The guttural voice gave Les the address. Les wrote it down and read it back.

'That is very good,' said the voice. 'I wish you luck. Now I must go. I will be in touch.'

'Hey listen . . .' said Les.

The line went dead. Les looked at his mobile, cleared it and left it on the kitchen table. Well, he thought, looking at the address, that's not far from here. I might leave the car and take my bike. That way no one can get my number, and I can still make a quick getaway if things happen to go pear shaped. Les started on his long neck again when he remembered something. He'd promised to ring Marla. Les got her phone number from his bag and rang on the land line. He got a voice message saying the phone was turned off. Les left a message then hung up. He took another swallow of beer and stared at the phone.

If he had any brains, he'd cook a steak and vegetables for tea. Lots of good, healthy protein and fibre. But Les couldn't be bothered. He flicked through the list of phone numbers he and Warren used frequently, found their favourite pizza delivery shop and ordered a large pizza marinara, ribs, wedges and salad. He was told it would be there within forty-five minutes. Les finished his beer, got another one and checked out the TV guide. There were two good back-to-back documentaries on SBS about the Israelis and the Arabs. Perfect, beamed Les. There's nothing like watching a lot of bloodshed, hatred, death and destruction on TV. And nobody can provide it with more panache, verve and flair than the Muslims and the Jews. Les settled back with his beer to watch the news and current affairs while he waited for his meal to arrive.

Les was halfway through a third beer and delirious with hunger when there was a knock on the door. He almost tore the cartons out of the delivery boy's hand when he paid him, then raced into the kitchen and attacked. When Les had finished the rib bones were shining like ivory and there was barely a grease mark left on the pizza carton. With his hunger pangs gone, Les made himself a delicious and settled back to watch the bombings and killing on TV.

The documentary turned out to be as grim and horrific as Les thought it would. Worse. Families were blown up on buses, bombs landed in people's houses, little kids got shot in the face with rubber bullets. And more. Les shook his head sadly as the credits rolled past. And the conspicuous compassion brigade want to put the boot into Australia all the time so they can give themselves a warm inner glow. None of us know how lucky we are to be living here. The evening wasn't a complete horror show, however. Les did get one laugh on the night.

SBS had gone commercial and they were rerunning one Warren had produced for a brand of soap called Lotus Flower. It featured two Polynesian drag queens built like front row forwards, standing at a bar in a disco. They both had faces like gorillas and the first one was telling the other the reason she had such a beautiful complexion was because she used Lotus Flower soap. Her big line was. 'Silly you,' because her friend wasn't using Lotus Flower. The commercial ended with the first drag queen leaving for the toilet, where she almost walks into the Gents. Instead, she turns to the camera, giggles, 'Silly me,' and walks into the Ladies. Les conceded to Warren it was a fairly humorous TV commercial. On the other hand, Warren had brought home a carton of Lotus Flower soap, and they were glad when it ran out, because both Les and Warren agreed it smelled like camel dung.

By now Les was on the nod. He was tired from the night before and after a run, a pizza, a few beers and the odd delicious, Les was looking forward to bed. He switched off the TV, cleaned up what little mess there was and shuffled to his bedroom. Les had barely pulled the duvet up round his chin and closed his eyes before he was gone.

The apartment at Ocean Star resort was definitely the lap of luxury. But as far as a country boy like Les was concerned, it was still nice to wake up in your own bed in your own home. Les yawned, stretched, did a couple of little, contented kicks, then reached across and drew back the vertical blind; although it was a little cool and cloudy outside, it was still a reasonably good day. Les pulled the duvet back round his ears and lay in bed for a while, then got up and went to the bathroom. His face hadn't improved any. But Les felt it wouldn't scare too many old ladies or little children, so when he finished, he put the kettle on, changed into his old grey tracksuit and strolled down to get the paper. Back in the kitchen he cooked some scrambled eggs and settled down to catch up on the news over breakfast. When Les had finished eating, he cleaned up and rang Marla again. This time she answered.

'Hello?'

'Marla. How are you? It's Les.'

'Les. Hey, how's things?'

'Pretty good. Are you at work?'

'Yes. But I can talk for a few minutes. I got your message. Did you get home all right?'

'Did I get home all right?' repeated Les. He gave Marla a quick run down about the trip home, including having to run it all out before he choked somebody. 'Fair dinkum. I was that hungry I would have eaten an elephant and chased the mahout.'

'Yes,' replied Marla. 'You get that every now and again, living on the Central Coast, Les.'

'It's still a nice part of the world though,' said Les.

'It is. Especially if you're staying in a squillion-dollar apartment overlooking the Haven,' said Marla.

'Yes. That helps,' agreed Les. 'So what's doing with the wallopers? Did you get another visit? Shit! I hate putting you through this.'

'That's okay,' said Marla. 'Yes. They called round again this afternoon. And like a good concerned citizen, I was able to help them with their enquiries.'

'Well done, Marla,' said Les. 'I'm proud of you. So what did you tell the dropkicks?'

'The truth,' replied Marla. 'I was drunk. You picked me up at the Point. Said your name was Larry or something and you ran a modelling agency in Sydney. You talked me into coming back to your place. And when you couldn't get into my pants, you threw me in a taxi and told me to piss off. A typical Aussie bloke.'

'Aren't men bastards,' chuckled Les.

'Tell me about it,' said Marla. 'But all jokes aside, Les, when I told them you were only defending both of us, they didn't want to believe me. So I think it was a good thing you went home.'

'Yeah. You're right,' Les nodded into the phone. 'But thanks for that Marla. I'll make it up to you.'

'You're a sweetheart. Listen, Les. I don't want to sound rude. But I'm up to my eyeballs in *Bindi the Bashful Bilby* at the moment. How about ringing me at home when I've got more time?'

'Sure.'

Les and Marla exchanged their home numbers and Les said he'd be in touch. After he hung up Les smiled at the phone. What a girl. Fair dinkum, if all the women on the Central Coast are anything like Marla, I'll move up there tomorrow. Les was gazing at the phone when another thought occurred to him. He'd better ring Eddie and tell the beastly little killer what happened. He'd try his mobile first. Eddie was there.

'Hello?'

'Eddie. It's Les.'

'Les. Hey, how's it going up in Terrigal?'

'It's not. I'm back in Bondi.'

'You're what?'

'Where are you?'

'Randwick,' replied Eddie. 'I just been doing something for Price.'

'Why don't you call round to my joint?' suggested Les.

'Righto,' said Eddie. 'See you in about fifteen.'

Les hung up and walked out to the backyard. He had time to bring in what little washing there was when there was a knock on the front door. Les opened it. Eddie was standing there wearing a black leather jacket over a brown check shirt and a pair of jeans.

'So what happened in Terrigal?' he asked, stepping inside as Les closed the door behind him.

'I give a couple of mugs a smack in the mouth,' replied Les.

'Is that what happened to your head?'

'No. That's another story. You want a coffee or something?'

'How about a sparkling mineral water?'

'Ice and slice, sir?'

'Of course. What do you think I am, a fuckin peasant?'

'Sorry,' apologised Les.

While he poured two large glasses of mineral water and added ice and a slice of lime, Les told Eddie what happened in Terrigal. They went into the loungeroom and Les explained to Eddie the reason his head looked a bit rough and everything else that had happened. When Les had finished Eddie didn't know whether to laugh or cry. All he could do was shake his head in disbelief.

'Jesus, you can get yourself into some bother,' said Eddie. 'You're un-fuckin-real.'

'I'm not bad, am I,' said Les.

'But what about that sheila Marla? How staunch was she, the way she handled the cops.'

'She was a good sort, too,' said Les.

Eddie eased back in his lounge chair. 'Billy already told me you were doing business with Menny Menjou. Looking for a film script or something.'

'That's right,' nodded Les. 'Nothing heavy. But it's worth fifty grand if I find it.'

'Fifty or five hundred, Les,' said Eddie, 'be careful with Menny. Or any of his team for that matter. They think mercy is French for thanks.'

'I'm aware of that,' said Les. 'But I've only really met one of his team. A big bloke called Lasjoz.'

'Lasjoz,' smiled Eddie. 'I'll tell you a funny story about him.'

'Oh. What's that?' asked Les.

'My missus gets her hair done in Oxford Street,' said Eddie, 'where she also likes to waste my money in the local boutiques.'

'As she's entitled to,' chided Les.

'Yeah, terrific. Anyway,' continued Eddie. 'She's spotted Lasjoz up there a few times. And she reckons he's Doris Day.'

'Lasjoz? Gay?' Les screwed his face up. 'Christ! He's eight foot tall. I watched him ride a Harley Davidson. And he threw it around like it was a Vespa scooter.'

'So?' shrugged Eddie. 'What about that big forward used to play for Souths? Remember when they were playing Manly and the fullback called him a poof. He knocked all his teeth out. They're still digging teeth up under the goal posts at Brookvale Oval.'

'Yeah, you're right,' said Les. 'Shit. Does Menny know this?'

'He wouldn't want to,' said Eddie. 'Menny's team are all Muslims. They hate poofs.'

'Well, I'll be buggered,' said Les.

'Don't say that in front of Lasjoz,' winked Eddie. 'He might have your pants off. And wooshka!'

'Ohh yuk!' grimaced Les. 'What a way to go.'

'A la carte,' smiled Eddie. 'So did you get your zinger?'

'Yeah,' answered Les. 'Did I what.'

'Have you tried it?'

'Reckon,' said Les. 'They're unreal.'

'They sure are.' Eddie leaned forward in his chair. 'Just between you, me and the gatepost, I had to pop a bloke a few weeks ago. You know Tuxedo Tovar?'

'That skinny Hungarian pain in the arse?' said Les.

'That's him. He lives, or lived, out at Rockdale. He came home. And I'm sitting in his loungeroom eating a peanut slab. He says, "Eddie. What you are doing here?" And I said. "Waiting for you to come home, Tovar, so I can shoot you. What you think I are doing here?" I put two in his clock and another in the back of his melon and left him there.'

'What about the body?' asked Les.

'Unless Tovar's smack-dealing mates haven't got rid of it by now,' shrugged Eddie, 'if it's not on the nose, it will definitely be on the turn.'

Les laced his hands across his chest. 'One thing about our line of work, Eddie. It never gets boring.'

'Never,' agreed Eddie. 'And whoever said crime doesn't pay should at least give it a go for a couple of weekends.'

'Exactly,' nodded Les.

Eddie rose to his feet. 'I have to make a move. But before I go, Price said to give you this.'

Eddie took a bulky envelope from the inside pocket of his leather jacket and tossed it to Les. Les caught it and felt the contents between his fingers.

'What's in here?' Les asked.

'Ten grand. Compliments of Barrow Boy.'

'Fuckin hell,' said Les. 'Is he a good bloke or what?'

'He also wants to know when you're coming back to work.'

'As soon as I can,' said Les, getting up out of his chair, before pointing to his face. 'But fair dinkum Eddie. How can I stand on the door with a melon like this? It'd turn you off a baked dinner.'

'Yeah, it's not the best,' agreed Eddie, as they walked back down the hallway. 'Okay. I'll see you, Les. Just remember what I said: be careful with Menny and his merry men.'

'I will,' said Les, opening the front door. He held up the envelope. 'And thanks for bringing this round.'

'No problemo, hombre.'

Les watched Eddie get inside his black Mercedes, then closed the front door and with a broad smile on his face, stashed the money in his wardrobe and walked back out to the kitchen. So what will I do now? Norton asked himself as he rinsed the two glasses. I wonder if Menny's having a coffee outside Azulejos? Probably. What I could do, is jog down there, say hello and carry on with a bit of bullshit about his missing film script. And whether he's there or not, keep on going. Les changed into his trainers and jogging gear, did a few stretches on the back verandah, then took off out the front door.

The council was still digging up the road when Les stopped at the bottom of Glenayr Avenue; the noise was just as bad, the air was still full of dust and the same girl from the council was running about with her STOP and GO sign directing traffic around the workers and concrete mixers. Bodene Menjou was seated in the same place with the two well-dressed men who turned up on Saturday morning plus another. There was no sign of Lasjoz or the women. Les removed his sunglasses and walked up to the well-dressed Bodene.

'Hello Menny,' said Les. 'How's things?'

'Les my friend,' said Bodene. 'How are you? By golly. From your face, very much in the wars I would say.'

'To be honest, Menny,' replied Les, 'I got all this looking for your script. I'm on the case, baby.'

'My word, you are good man,' Bodene answered sincerely. 'I knew I could trust you. You want coffee or drink?'

'No thanks mate,' answered Les. 'I'm in the middle of a run.'

'You like to keep fit, Les. Is good,' smiled Bodene. 'But before we go on. There has been new development with missing film script.'

'There has?' said Les.

'Yes. Some piece of shit rings up and says he has script. But for it he wants one hundred thousand dollar. Bastard.'

'What? Tell him to get stuffed. He's trying to rip you off. I'm still a good chance of finding it yet.'

'Not only that,' Bodene screwed up his face, 'the bastard who rings me sounded like poofter.'

'A horse's hoof? You're kidding, Menny.'

'Is truth,' snorted Bodene.

'So what did you do?' asked Les.

'I tell him, get fucked poofter bastard,' said Bodene. 'I hate poofters. Back in my country we give them Gay Mardi Gras and rave party. We cut their throats. Is right, Harun?'

'Is right for sure,' nodded the Albanian seated on Bodene's right.

'One hundred per cent,' grunted the man seated next to him. 'Fuck poofters. Same for Elton John and Boy George. Fancy pants bastards.'

'Fair enough,' said Les. 'But Menny, there's one thing I wanted to ask you.'

'Sure, Les. Anything, my friend,' replied the Albanian gangster.

'When your script got stolen from outside your restaurant, who was there?'

'Who was there?' replied Bodene. 'I must think. Lasjoz. Little Sakchej. Emolich. Topaz and Barbara. Shop was not open. Why you ask?'

'Oh nothing,' answered Les. 'I was just curious. That's all.' A council worker started up with a jack hammer. Les put his sunnies back on and smiled at Bodene. 'Anyway. I'll keep going.' He pointed at Bodene. 'Don't pay the person that rang you. Leave it with me. Okay?'

'Les,' said Bodene. 'I am trusting you. Like I trust my own mother.'

'Good. I'll be in touch. See you, Menny. See you, fellahs.'

To several grunted goodbyes, Les left Menny and his friends and continued on up Warners Avenue. He did a lap of the golf links, and when he got home cranked out a few crunches and threw the kettlebell around before having a shower.

Well, that's a turn up for the books, mused Les as he changed into a clean grey T-shirt and his blue cargoes. Big Lasjoz could be batting for the other side, and some poof's rung Bodene wanting a hundred grand for his script. Christ! I wouldn't like to be in their shoes if Menny ever finds out who it is. In the meantime, my connection has told me the script's in a house down the road. Les looked at his watch. Bloody hell! Where's the day gone? By the time I get a bite to eat, it'll be time to go round and play cat burglars. Les wiped his sunglasses clean, put his tracksuit top on and walked down to the Hakoah Club.

After a T-bone steak, vegetables, mudcake and two flat whites, Les felt reasonably contented. He strolled home, putsed around the house for a while, then took his push-bike from the back verandah. He was about to get his zinger and a couple of other things from his bedroom, when his mobile rang on the kitchen table.

'Hello?'

'Hello Les. It's Topaz. Remember me?'

'Topaz. Yeah, Barbara's girlfriend from Saturday morning. Of course I remember you,' Les smiled into the phone. 'How are you?'

'I'm good,' replied Topaz. 'How's yourself?'

'Oh, can't complain,' answered Les. 'Did Bodene give you my number?'

'That's right. I hope you don't mind me ringing you?'

'No. Not at all,' said Les. 'It's really nice of you. I'm flattered.'

'Thank you.'

'So how come you decided to give me a call?'

'Oh, Bodene talks about you. So does Barbara. You sound like an interesting person.'

'Well. I'd rather be an interesting person than a person of interest, as they say.'

'Yes,' chuckled Topaz. 'You get a few of them hanging around with Bodene and his friends.'

'I would imagine,' said Les. 'So where are you ringing from? Work?'

'That's right.'

'What do you do?'

'I work at the Blue Adriatic Travel Agency for an associate of Bodene's.'

'The Blue Adriatic Travel Agency,' smiled Les. 'I imagine one-way tickets back to Albania would be on special there, Topaz.'

'All the time,' replied Topaz. 'What kind of passport would you prefer? Irish and Canadian are very popular. New Zealand is good.'

'No, that's quite all right,' said Les. 'My good old Aussie one will do me for the time being.'

'Well, just let me know if ever you should change your mind. I can also arrange plastic surgery in Thailand. And a good deal on American Express traveller's cheques from Hong Kong.'

'Thanks, Topaz. I'll remember that. Hey, this might sound funny,' said Les, 'but when I saw you with Bodene on Saturday morning, I thought you might have been Lasjoz's girlfriend.'

'What?' exclaimed Topaz. 'God! Give me a break. Have you ever seen him with his shirt off? He needs a flea collar.'

'Well, I don't know these things,' explained Les.

'What about you, Les. Have you got a girlfriend?'

Les shook his head. 'No. I haven't even got a cat. Or a budgerigar. Not even a goldfish.'

'Don't you get lonely?'

'All the time, Topaz. It's awful. I've even joined a poets' circle. Would you like me to read you some of my works?'

'I don't know,' replied Topaz. 'Are they any good?'

'Reckon,' said Les. 'I've been told my "Ode to Epsom Salts" is very moving indeed.'

'Wow! I'm moved already.'

'Thanks.'

'So how are you going with your search for Bodene's missing film script?' asked Topaz.

'Sort of all right,' answered Les. 'I'm onto a couple of things.'

'You get around, don't you?'

'Not really, Topaz. I just know a lot of the wrong kind of people from work. That's all.'

'I can understand that,' said Topaz. 'Les. What are you doing tomorrow?'

'Thursday. Nothing really. Why?'

'Barbara's getting her hair done in the morning, at Bondi. And we're going for coffee afterwards. I was wondering if you might like to join us?'

'I'd love to, Topaz,' replied Norton. 'What time and whereabouts?'

'Say ten thirty, elevenish. At Gabrielle's and Liza's.'

'Ohh, even better,' said Les. 'I go there all the time. In fact I think I've seen you in there.'

'I've seen you too. You like to sit on that lounge in the middle room.'

'That's right. Sometimes I meet up with some friends from work.'

The line went quiet for a moment. 'Les. I have to go, the other phone's ringing. I'll see you tomorrow.'

'Okay. See you then.'

Les hung up and stared at his mobile sitting on the kitchen table. Well, how about that. What did Rose say? Expect the unexpected. Coffee tomorrow could be very interesting. Especially with Barbara Beauty Spot in the company. She is a rocket salad. Now, where was I? Planning a burglary.

Les wheeled his push-bike out onto the verandah, got a couple of things from his bedroom, then locked the front door behind him. After adjusting his sunglasses, he slipped on a pair of gloves, took his bike out the front, then spread his backside across the saddle and pedalled off.

After exiting his street, Lamrock Avenue was downhill all the way and Les soon coasted to a stop in front of the address Deep Throat had given him: a narrow semi with a red gate and a low brick fence out front, just back from Chambers Avenue.

The semi was painted off-white and kept very neat with a small verandah and two windows facing the street. On the right was a side passage with a metal security gate. Les had a quick look around, opened the front gate and wheeled his bike across the yard and left it against the security gate. Convinced no one had seen him, he walked back and knocked on the front door. After knocking twice more and getting no answer, Les removed his sunglasses and took the zinger from his pocket. There were two locks on the door; the zinger whirred twice and Les was inside.

Despite the villain inside him, Norton wasn't used to this and it didn't feel right being inside someone else's home without them knowing. The sooner he got his 'dirty deed done dirt cheap' finished and was out of there, the better. Les wrapped a blue bandana around his face, flicked on a small torch and started looking around.

It was a basic, restored, old Bondi semi. Two bedrooms and a bathroom on the right faced a narrow, blue-carpeted hallway that ran down to a small loungeroom with a piano in one corner. There was a dining room with a small kitchen alongside and a locked and bolted door led to an enclosed verandah and a small backyard. The furnishings were tasteful and modern with a blue velvet lounge, framed prints on the walls, plenty of bric-a-brac and several frilly lampshades. A huge panda bear sporting a pink cowboy hat sprawled in the corner of the blue velvet lounge. Les decided to take a preliminary look in the front bedroom, work his way down to the dining room and if he didn't find the bag the first time, start again and give the place a good going over.

Creeping slowly back along the hallway, Les could swear every creaking floorboard under his feet was screaming its head off that there was an intruder in the house, till he got to the front bedroom and flicked his torch around. A double bed with a white duvet and several fluffy dolls sat between the front windows and a dressing table. A sideboard sat against another wall, next to a built-in wardrobe with mirrors across the front. On top of the sideboard were four handbags. One was crocodile skin, but none were green. Les slid the door back on the wardrobe. Amongst the dresses and tops were two men's suits and two pairs of men's shoes. The lady must have a gentleman visitor, smiled Les as he closed the door. He flashed the torch around then moved on to the next bedroom.

It too had built-in wardrobes and a dressing table and a sideboard. But only a single bed stood beneath a window opening onto the side passage. Like the front room, several handbags sat on the sideboard; however, not a green one in sight. There were also men's clothes hanging up in the wardrobe amongst the dresses and slacks. Shit, thought Les. The boyfriend must get a bit cramped spending the night in a single bed. He left the bedroom and proceeded on to the loungeroom, stopping for a quick look in the bathroom.

The bathroom was neat and fairly tidy, with a white plastic shower screen covered in coloured ducks and a pair of scales under the sink covered in talcum powder. Sitting amongst the toothbrushes and soap, on a glass shelf above the sink, were two plastic men's razors and two electric ones. Plus two bottles of expensive men's aftershave amongst the women's perfume. Looks like the boyfriends have certainly settled in, mused Les. Half their luck. Les left the bathroom and stepped out into the hallway, where his stomach suddenly turned to ice. The front door opened and two people stepped inside.

'Well, how would I know whose bike it is, Lola?' said one voice. 'It's certainly not mine, or anyone I know.'

'It's a man's bike, too, Chontelle,' said the other voice.

'Somebody must have ...'

The door closed, Les turned towards it and his torch picked up two of the biggest women Les had ever seen in his life. The first one, Chontelle, had braided blonde hair stacked around a face with a wheelbarrow of make-up caked on it and she was wearing a black dress, high heels and fishnet stockings. Lola had a thick black Afro, the same amount of make-up, plus a huge pair of false eyelashes and looked quite tidy in a maroon slack suit and matching Doc Marten shoes. The two women stared down the hallway, turned to each other then glared daggers at Les.

'And just who the hell are you?' demanded Chontelle.

Les gestured helplessly. 'Ladies,' he tried to explain. 'It's not quite what you think.'

'It's a bloody burglar,' howled Lola.

'Get him, Lola. The thieving bastard,' hissed Chontelle. 'He'll be sorry he broke into our house.'

'Look girls. Will you just let me ...'

It was too late. Chontelle kicked off her high heels and the two women tore down the hallway and crash-tackled Les with a hit as hard as any he'd felt playing first grade rugby league. Les yelped as the torch went up in the air and he was swept off his feet and sent flying back into the loungeroom, banging his head on a chair hard enough to make him see stars. Next thing Les knew, he was being punched and kicked all round the loungeroom floor with frightening ferocity. One well-aimed kick from Lola's Doc Martens caught him above the left eye, tearing open the flesh. As his eye filled with blood, Les felt a vase get smashed over the top of his head and he saw more stars. Shit, sweated Les, I got to do something here or I'm going to finish up topside fuckin mince.

Chontelle was standing over him, so Les shoved his hand up her dress to grab her pubic hairs and start yanking on them. But instead of getting a fist full of ted, Les was shocked to find his hand wrapped round a huge pair of balls and fairly decent length of pipe. Despite his initial horror, Les yanked on everything anyway. Chontelle screamed and bent down to grab Norton's hand, accidentally elbowing Lola in the face and temporarily stopping her from bashing into Les. This was all the breathing space Norton needed. He forced himself up between the two huge drag queens, grabbed Lola by her Afro and Chontelle by her braids and banged their heads together; once, twice and a third time for luck.

The two drag queens had big, hard heads and it wasn't enough to knock them out. But it gave Les time to break free. Up on his feet, he could have started punching and kicking into the two stunned drag queens and gained the upper hand. But Les knew he was in the wrong and they were entitled to give him a good hiding after catching him inside their house. Les left them and sped off down the hallway, tearing open the front door before slamming it shut behind him. After a quick look around, Les quickly re-tied the bandana across his forehead to stop the blood running into his eyes, then got on his push-bike and went for his life back up Lamrock Avenue, standing up on the pedals and wrenching the handlebars towards him like he was overtaking the field in the Tour de France.

Mrs Curtin was pottering about in her small garden across the road and didn't see Les when he pulled up in front of his house. He ran up the stairs, dumped his bike on the verandah and quickly opened the front door. Once inside, Les hurried straight to the bathroom.

'Oh, fuck me dead,' Les wailed when he removed the blood-soaked bandana and looked at himself in the mirror. 'What next?'

Norton was a mess. His hair was full of blood from the cut he got when the vase was broken over his head, blood was running down his face from the cut above his eye, his face had been pummelled and his teeth were chipped. Besides that, his back felt like he'd just woken up after spending the night sleeping on a pile of blue metal. This time he needed medical attention. Les threw his bandana in the shower, filled the sink full of warm water and washed most of the blood away. He then wrapped a towel round his head, walked out to the phone in the loungeroom and dialled.

'Hello. Dr Kenneth's surgery.'

'Hello Anjuska. It's Les Norton.'

'Oh hello, Les. How are you?'

'I'm in a spot of bother actually.'

'Is it an emergency, Les?'

'Yeah. I cut my head open and I'm bleeding all over the place.'

'All right, Les,' said Anjuska. 'Come straight over. There's a few waiting, but Greg will be with you as soon as he can.'

'Thanks, Anjuska. I'll be there in a few minutes.'

Les hung up then changed the towel around his head along with his blood-soaked clothes and into a clean black T-shirt and black cargoes to hide any blood. He got his wallet, then left the house and headed for Dr Kenneth's surgery opposite the golf links in Old South Head Road. As he drove there, Les reflected on Dr Gregory Kenneth.

Greg was an old GPS boy and he and his Russian-born wife, Anjuska, were Eastern Suburbs royalty. He dressed immaculately and was an old mate of Price's, and he'd been looking after the team at the Kelly Club for years; Les had just been there to get treatment for his flu. Dr Kenneth wouldn't do anything illegal, like remove bullets; Eddie had an old medic mate from Vietnam who did that. But Greg knew what their line of work involved and was always available to tend their various wounds, patch them up and get them on their way. Greg was losing his hair and always got around with a world-weary smile on his face. But he had such a soothing, reassuring manner, it almost made being sick a pleasure. That, however, was Greg's good side. There were plenty of times the boys could have easily choked Dr Kenneth with his stethoscope.

As well as his soothing manner, Dr Kenneth had a bestial, dry sense of humour and liked nothing better than to guilefully sucker the boys into an irrelevant conversation, then hit them with a vicious pun at the end that left them feeling like complete dills. And he rarely missed.

Les found a parking spot at the end of Blair Street, walked round to the surgery, through the gate out front and pushed open the glass door. The surgery was like most doctors' practices:

a waiting room on the left, a corridor with the consulting rooms in the middle and the reception on the right. There was a smattering of people seated round the waiting room, Anjuska was behind the desk in a white dress with her dark hair perfectly coiffured, and standing next to her was Lin, their Malaysian nurse, in a starched blue uniform.

'Oh dear, Les,' said Anjuska as Les walked up to the desk. 'You have been in the wars, haven't you?'

'I've seen better days,' agreed Les.

'You were only up here last week.'

'Yeah. I can't keep away from the place. It's Greg's bedside manner.'

Anjuska turned to the nurse. 'Lin. Take Les into the first room and prep him till Greg's available.'

'All right, Mrs Kenneth,' replied the nurse. 'This way, Mr Norton.'

'Thanks.'

Holding the towel round his head, Les followed Lin into the first consulting room where she got him to lie down on the rubber bench and removed the towel. She put a pair of latex gloves on and rinsed the two cuts in Norton's head, then told him to keep the towel on till Greg was ready. Les did as he was told and settled back to peer at the posters and other odds and ends in the consulting room. After all the excitement he was starting to relax when Greg walked in wearing a pair of dark blue trousers, a light blue shirt and a lemon cashmere cardigan. Lin was behind him.

'Hello, Les,' he said, rubbing his hands together. 'How are you, mate?'

Les removed the towel. 'How do I look, Greg?'

'Best I've seen you looking for ages,' said Dr Kenneth, examining the cuts. 'How did all this happen?'

That was another thing the boys hated about Greg. You could never lie to him. 'I got jumped by a couple of giant drag queens,' said Les. 'One kicked me in the face. The other broke a vase over my head.'

'You weren't trying to steal their handbags, were you, Les?'

Les closed his eyes. 'Funny you should say that, Greg. But indirectly, that had something to do with it.'

'There's some other lacerations, too,' noticed Dr Kenneth. 'Smaller ones. Where did they come from?'

'Three crazy women attacked me with broomsticks,' answered Les.

'Three crazy women attacked you with broomsticks. What were you trying to steal from them?'

'Indirectly again, Greg. The same handbag.'

'The same handbag,' repeated Dr Kenneth. 'That's very good, Les. All right, Lin. Shave the hair around the cut on Mr Norton's scone. Then give him a local. Do you want a local Les?' Dr Kenneth asked.

'Yes please,' replied Norton. 'And plenty of it.'

'Get the big needle, Lin. Clean the rust off with a bit of steel wool.'

Dr Kenneth left the room. Lin got a pair of clippers and removed the hair around the cut on the top of Norton's head. She left his eyebrow, then got a needle and loaded it up.

'This might sting a little Mr Norton,' she said.

'Good,' replied Les. 'I deserve it.'

It stung; then everything settled down. The bleeding eased and in the peace and quiet of the surgery, Les began to chill out. Dr Kenneth returned, put on a pair of latex gloves and started suturing Norton's scalp. He softly talked about the weather, Price's photo in the paper, asked Les how his flu was. Five stitches later, Dr Kenneth started on Norton's eye.

'Funny you should mention drag queens,' said the good doctor as he put the first stitch in. 'I'm treating a lesbian from up the Cross at the moment. You might know her.'

'Yeah?' replied Les, his eyes closed, breathing deeply and totally relaxed under Dr Kenneth's soothing manner.

'She's an exotic dancer. Calls herself Kitty Littah.'

'Kitty Littah?' said Les. 'Can't say I've heard of her.'

'Fair enough.' Dr Kenneth snipped the suture. 'I thought you might have. That's all.'

Norton's curiosity was aroused. 'What are you treating her for? Am I allowed to ask?'

'Sure. Just a tiny bit of thrush. That's all. Barely noticeable.'

'Right,' said Les, sleepily.

'But I have to tell you something, Les,' said Dr Kenneth. 'This woman has got the cleanest vagina I have ever seen. Ever.'

'A clean ted?' said Les.

'Exceptional, Les. I've never seen anything like it. You could eat your dinner off it. The Pope could serve holy communion on it. It's absolutely amazing.'

'Really.'

Dr Kenneth put in another stitch. 'When I was an intern, I was in gynaecology for a while. And I can tell you, Les, I've seen plenty of fannies in my time. But this one is absolutely outstanding.'

Les stifled a yawn. 'It must be to impress you, Greg.'

'So being a doctor and into hygiene and all that,' said Dr Kenneth, 'I had to find out her secret. So I asked her. I said, your vagina is an absolute credit to you. How do you keep it so clean?'

'And what did she say?' asked Les.

'She said she has a woman in twice a week.'

'Ohh, piss off will you, Greg,' moaned Les. 'Can't you see I'm in enough pain and suffering as it is?'

'And you're going to be in a lot more tonight,' smiled the good doctor, snipping the fourth and last stitch. 'So I'm giving you a script for some Panadeine Forte and Valium. When these kick in, you're going to love me, Les.'

'Don't you believe it.'

'All right, Lin. Bandage Mr Norton up. Escort him to the front desk and tell Anjuska to take his money.' Dr Kenneth patted Les on the shoulder. 'Take it easy for the time being, Les. Then I'll see you in a week and remove the stitches.'

'Okay, Greg.' Les smiled and shook Dr Kenneth's hand. 'Thanks a lot, mate.'

Lin put dressing plasters on Norton's head and eye, then he picked his script up at the desk, produced his Visa card and paid the gap. After thanking Lin and Anjuska, Les walked back to his car and drove home, stopping in Hall Street to pick up his medication. Half an hour later it was dark and Les was home sipping a cup of tea in the kitchen.

Well, that was another good day fucked, moped Les, staring out the kitchen window at the house next door. I know one thing: if that rotten bloody Deep Throat rings me again, I'll tell him to go fuck himself.

Suddenly Norton's eyes narrowed. No I won't. I'll arrange to meet the bastard somewhere. Then I'll give him a bit of what those two Tootsies gave me. Les stared out the window a while longer. He didn't feel hungry. What he felt like was a nice, relaxing hot bath. He finished his tea and left the mug in the sink.

Les ran a bath, tipped in half a packet of Radox, then slowly lowered his bruised and battered body into the water. It felt divine. Soon all the aches and pains in his back eased and Les almost fell asleep from sheer bliss. After a good long soak, Les got out, had a shave then changed into a clean white T-shirt under his dark blue tracksuit and walked out to the kitchen.

His back felt better. But his head was aching and the stitches hurt if he made any sudden movements. An uncomfortable thought suddenly occurred to Les. What was he going to tell Price and the rest of them? They were expecting him back at the club next week. Les noticed his pills sitting where he'd left them on the kitchen table. He made himself a delicious then washed down two Valium and two Panadeine Forte and checked the TV guide. There was a half good show on SBS about ancient Rome. Les settled down in front of the TV and sipped his delicious.

Another delicious and around thirty minutes into the show, the pills kicked in and Les turned into a big, happy, smiling beach ball. There was no pain. There was no nothing. If the Radox bath was bliss, this was bliss immaculate. Les didn't give a stuff about anything. If a UFO landed in the backyard and an alien walked into the loungeroom, Les wouldn't have moved. He would simply have smiled and said, 'Hello, little green man. Nice to see you. Have a few Vs dude.' Les dissolved into the lounge and gazed vacantly at the giant-screen TV. He was gazing away when the ad for Lotus Flower soap came on. Les stared at the TV, then closed his eyes for a moment and shook his head. No, he told himself, that can't possibly be right. I'm seeing things. Through Norton's sedated eyes, the two big drag queens in the commercial were the same ones who gave him the serve earlier. Chontelle and Lola. Even the voices sounded the same. Les stared at the TV in disbelief right up until Chontelle uttered her line outside the toilet. No, Les told himself. It's the Valium.

By the time the show ended, Les was almost out to it on the lounge. He left his glass where it was, turned off the TV and the lights and drifted to his room through a beautiful fog of peaceful, tranquil, all-embracing nothingess. He managed to knot a bandana around his head, then smiling blankly round his room, doused the lights and crawled into his soft, warm bed. Les was asleep before he could pull the duvet up under his chin.

When Norton woke up the next morning, the pills had worn off and the big Queenslander was back to the real world. His head was sore and he could feel the stitches where they tightened on his scalp and above his eye. When he swung his legs out of bed and stood up, Les could also feel where every kick and punch had landed on his body. There would be no running or hitting the heavy bag today. He went to the bathroom, removed the bandana and stared at himself in the mirror. If his head looked rough before, now he could add another, much bigger black eye and more bruising. And I've got to meet Topaz and Barbara later, mused Les. That's going to be nice. The only small consolation was, when he ran a finger round inside his mouth, the chips in his teeth weren't as bad as he first thought.

'So how are you going there, tough guy?' Les asked the reflection smiling mirthlessly back at him in the mirror. 'What did you say? You got beaten up by three old sheilas with broomsticks and two drag queens. Shit! You are a tough guy, aren't you. You fuckin moron.'

After finishing in the bathroom, Les walked out to the kitchen. He'd had a good night's sleep and apart from some stiffness he didn't feel lethargic. He still wasn't that hungry. But he had to eat something. Les put the kettle on and sorted out some poached eggs on toast.

A light breakfast perked Les up even more. He would have enjoyed some exercise. But he'd only tear the stitches. Outside it was quite a nice day, cool and sunny with a light westerly. A nice long walk where no one could see him would be ideal. Les climbed into his old grey tracksuit and trainers, got his sunglasses and drove down to Centennial Park.

Les walked for well over an hour, not thinking about much, mostly taking in the surroundings, nodding to a few joggers, other walkers and any rangers on horseback. It was quite enjoyable out in the sun, amongst the trees and flowers with the birds swooping about or paddling around in the ponds. A couple of things entered his mind about Bodene's missing script that could be worth looking into. Like the mysterious gay bloke ringing Bodene. Les pondered who that might be. And who was bloody Deep Throat? Could it possibly be one of the three men seated with Bodene the day before? It was all getting a little weird. Les was also thinking of giving the whole idea a complete miss. It certainly hadn't brought him much joy so far. But fifty grand was fifty grand. And Rose the tarot lady said he'd be rewarded, and she'd been pretty much on the money so far.

When he'd finished walking, Les drove home and managed to have a shower without getting the stitches wet. As he was towelling off, he could feel the walk had taken a lot of the stiffness out of his back and legs. After several glasses of water, Les changed into his blue cargoes, a white T-shirt he had bought in Hawaii, and a black baseball cap. By now he was ready to kill for a cup of coffee. He wiped his sunglasses, shrugged indifferently at the battered face looking back at him in the bedroom mirror, threw his blue tracksuit top over his shoulder, locked the house and walked down to Gabrielle's and Liza's.

The staff and the owner gave Les an inquisitive greeting when he walked in. Topaz and Barbara were seated at the lounge in the middle room where Les liked to sit, both wearing lots of freshly ironed denim and tasteful bling. Barbara's blonde hair was combed down with tiny blue tips here and there and looked extra good. Which didn't stop Les as he smiled and walked up to their table.

'Shit! What happened, Barbara?' he asked. 'I thought you were getting your hair done. Were they closed?'

Barbara ignored Les as she and Topaz stared at him. 'Les,' said Barbara. 'Take your sunglasses off.'

'Sure.'

Both Topaz and Barbara gave a little gasp. 'Good lord,' said Topaz. 'Who gave you that?'

Les took his cap off and bent his head down. 'The same people that gave me this.'

'My God,' said Barbara.

Les put his cap back on and sat down next to Barbara. 'Well. What's up?' he asked as the two girls continued to stare at him. 'Haven't you ever seen a bloke with two black eyes and stitches in his head before?'

'Not one I've arranged to meet for coffee,' said Topaz.

'Would you like to see some more?' said Les. He lifted up his T-shirt and showed the girls some of the bruises around his chest and ribs. 'You like the pattern?'

'Holy cow,' said Barbara.

'Actually,' said Les. 'I got this sticking up for you, Beauty Spot.'

'For me?' said Barbara.

'Yeah. I bumped into some blokes last night. And one of them reckoned you weren't fit to live in a shit house.'

'What? Who said this?' demanded Barbara.

'Some bloke,' shrugged Les. 'Anyway. I reckoned you were. And it sort of carried on from there.'

'Les,' said Barbara. 'I might be dumb. But I'm not stupid. What really happened? Christ! When I was working up the club, you were Captain Invincible.'

'Yeah? Well, Captain Invincible met Kommandant Kryptonite and his offsider.' The waiter came over and Les ordered a latte. 'You girls right for coffee?' Les asked.

'I'll have another flat white,' said Barbara.

'Yes. Me too,' said Topaz.

'Make that one latte and two flat whites, thanks.'

'No problem,' said the waiter.

'So what really happened, Les?' asked Topaz. 'Is it okay to ask?'

Les drummed his fingers on the table. 'What I tell you stays between the three of us. Okay?'

'Sure,' nodded Barbara.

'I got this looking for Bodene's film script.'

While they waited for the coffees, Les gave the girls a watered-down version of what happened. He didn't mention the zinger or his trip up to the Central Coast. The coffees arrived, Les sugared his and took an appreciative sip. 'So that's about it, ladies,' he said nonchalantly. 'You have your good days and you have your bad days. And that was one of them.'

'Cripes. Was it what,' said Topaz.

'My God!' laughed Barbara. 'Les Norton, getting beaten up by drag queens and old ladies with broomsticks. Where will it all end?'

'Who knows, Barbara,' said Les, taking a sip of coffee. 'Anyway. Let's change the subject. How are you and Bodene getting along?'

'Good,' nodded Barbara. 'Sometimes I think I might have made a wrong mistake going out with him. But he looks after me.'

'That's good,' said Les. 'I just hope a solid citizen like Menny doesn't find out about your previous indiscretions in London, Barbara.'

Barbara fluttered her eyelids at Norton. 'Les,' she insisted. 'I did not commit a crime in London. I simply failed to comply with the law. That's all.'

'Menny a solid citizen?' said Topaz. 'Christ! Him and his friends are that crooked, if they ate nails, they'd shit corkscews.'

'I don't think he'd like to hear you saying that, Topaz,' smiled Les.

'No,' said Barbara. 'Bodene's got a wonderful expression: dead fish don't swim against the current.'

'Eddie hasn't got a bad one either,' said Les. 'In order for three people to keep a secret, two have got to be dead.'

More coffees arrived, Les ordered a piece of cheesecake and they chit chatted about different things. It turned out Topaz lived at Rose Bay with her Maltese mother. She was an old SCEGGS girl, had a degree in pharmacy from Sydney University and was a fully qualified chemist. But she could earn more money working for Bodene's Albanian friends in the travel agency.

'Are you working for the friendly Albanians too, Barbara?' Les asked.

Barbara nodded. 'Yes. I help Bodene run the pizza shop. Do the ordering and the books and that.'

'Cool,' Les nodded back.

'We're no more than a couple of hard-working shop assistants,' smiled Topaz.

'Sounds like it,' said Les, returning Topaz's smile. He took a sip of coffee and placed his cup down. 'You know, there's something I have to ask you girls.'

'Sure. What's that Les?' answered Barbara.

'Lasjoz,' said Les. 'Is he ...?' Les gestured with one hand. 'Is he a bit Doris?'

The girls exchanged quick glances and Les didn't have to be psychic to read *Yes, he is*, and *How did you know?* in their eyes.

'Lasjoz, gay?' replied Barbara. 'Not a chance.'

'No,' added Topaz. 'He's as straight as they come. He's always trying to hit on me.'

'Fair enough,' said Les. 'I was just curious. Some friends of mine saw him up Oxford Street a few times, that's all. Does he live up there?' Les enquired.

'No. He lives in Bondi,' said Barbara. 'In Curlewis Street. The block of flats next to the car wash.'

'Right,' nodded Les.

Barbara nodded to Norton's head. 'Since you got bashed up by those two Tootsies, you're seeing poofs everywhere, Les.'

'You're probably right, Barbara,' agreed Les. 'I'm developing a creeping homophobic paranoia.'

Topaz glanced at her watch. 'We might have to get going soon, Barbara,' she declared.

Barbara glanced at her watch also. 'Yes, you're right, Topaz. Golly. Where did the time go?'

Topaz turned to Norton. 'What are you doing tonight, Les?' she asked.

Les pointed to his black eyes. 'With a face like this, what do you think? Staying home where no one can see me.'

'Yeah, you're not wrong,' agreed Barbara. 'It'd scare a buzzard off a shit cart.'

'How would you like me to come over and cook tea for you?' asked Topaz. 'And we could watch a DVD.'

Les couldn't believe his luck. He intended getting Topaz's phone number and asking her out when his face healed up. 'That would be lovely, Topaz,' he replied. 'I'd like that very much.'

'Better still,' said Topaz. 'I'll bring you over some of my mother's chicken soup and banana-rhubarb pie.'

'You got me,' beamed Les.

'About seven, seven thirtyish?'

'That would be great.'

'I might catch a taxi and we can have a few drinks.'

'Do that,' said Les. 'I'll pay for it.'

'No. That's okay,' said Topaz.

'Okay. Well at least let me shout the coffees.'

Les paid for the coffees, cheesecake and bagels. Barbara was parked in Consett Avenue. Les said he'd walk down to the corner with them, then go and have a look at the ocean. He gave Topaz his address, told her he'd see her that night, said goodbye at the corner and continued on to Campbell Parade.

There were no shortage of people eating or walking around Bondi enjoying the day when Les got there, and although the westerly had blown the surf out, a pocket of waxheads were jammed in the corner at the south end of the beach, surfing the most miniscule break imaginable. After all the coffee he'd drunk, Norton's mouth felt gluggy, so he thought he'd have a mineral water. He was standing outside Ravesi's and the bar wasn't crowded. Les stepped inside and got a middy of mineral water, ice and slice. He found a stool where the windows opened onto Campbell Parade and sat there sipping his mineral water while he checked out the punters.

Les was perving on a young Brazilian girl walking past, who had somehow managed to squeeze her heartbreak behind into an incredibly tight pair of cut-down jeans, and he didn't notice a tall man with straight brown hair and a straight face approach him on the right. The man was wearing a blue suit, matching tie and sunglasses, and although he appeared fairly nondescript, the way the man moved amongst the backpackers and local street freaks, it didn't take long to figure out he was a cop.

'Hello, Les,' said the man in the blue suit. 'How are you?'

Les slowly moved his eyes away from the young girl's behind and looked up. 'Hey, Rod,' he smiled. 'How are you, mate?'

'Not bad. What are you doing?'

Les nodded to the girl disappearing amongst the crowd along Campbell Parade. 'I was just watching that sensational little arse go past. I nearly fell off my stool.'

'Yeah,' agreed Rod. 'I've been tailing her since the Biltmore Hotel. It's something else, isn't it?'

The man in the blue suit was Detective Rod Maroney, a good, straight-up cop from Bondi police station. He was an old friend of Billy Dunne's since school, and like Billy, he wasn't a bad amateur light-heavyweight boxer before he joined the police force. Now Rod's kids played soccer with Billy's and their wives went shopping together. He knew Les and the team and most of what they got up to and as far as Rod was concerned, what he didn't know about them wouldn't hurt him. They might not have been one hundred per cent solid citizens, but they weren't drug dealers, rapists or armed hold-up merchants and they certainly didn't steal old lady's handbags. In fact the boys had helped Rod nick a few lowlifes that needed nicking badly for everybody's good.

'So what's happening, Rod, old son?' asked Les. 'You out there patrolling the parks and streets, making sure they're safe for people to take their drugs in?'

'I'm doing everything I can to ensure that, Les,' smiled Rod. The smile vanished and he tapped the window sill in front of where Les was seated. 'Listen, Les,' he said, seriously. 'I shouldn't be telling you this, but I'm going to give you some real good advice.'

'Sure,' said Les, seriously.

'Don't be seen hanging around Azulejos with Bodene Menjou.'

'Yeah?'

'Yeah,' nodded Detective Maroney. 'Keep right away from that lowlife Albanian dropkick. And his friends too.'

'Okay,' replied Les. 'But I haven't been ...'

'I don't care what you've been doing, Les,' cut in Rod. 'Just keep away from the prick.'

'Okay,' nodded Les.

'And those two sheilas. Barbara Lewis and Topaz Delimara. Play them wide, too.'

'I just had a coffee with them up the road,' said Les. 'I know Barbara from when she used to work at the club.'

'Yeah. Well, make that your last coffee with them,' advised Rod.

'Okay. Fair enough, Rod,' said Les.

'Now I have to get back to work.' Detective Maroney pushed his sunglasses down over the bridge of his nose and smiled. 'And like they say in your line of work, Les, if anyone asks, you haven't seen me. All right.'

'Say nothin' to nobody,' Les replied out the side of his mouth.

'Exactly.'

'All right. See you, Rod.' Les raised his glass. 'And thanks for the tip.'

'No worries, Les.'

Norton watched Detective Maroney walk off and continued sipping his mineral water. So. Rod must have seen me down there with Bodene on Saturday morning and thought I was up to something. Surely he knows me better than that. As for Topaz and Barbara, Topaz I don't know. And apart from having a shonky boyfriend, Barbara's harmless. Anyway, despite Rod's advice, smiled Les, a sequence of events has been put into action that is impossible to stop. Topaz is calling round my place tonight with homemade chicken soup. And even if she's running a terrorist network, she's a good sort and I love homemade chicken soup. Nevertheless, concluded Norton, this whole missing bag thing is getting a bit weird. And the sooner I knock it on the head the better. Fifty grand or no fifty grand. Tarot cards or no tarot cards. But before I do, I might poke my head into one more nook and cranny. Lasjoz was there when the script went missing. There's a chance he might have cooked up a scheme to nick Bodene's script, and used one of his poof mates as a go-between. Les finished his mineral water, left Ravesi's and walked down to Curlewis Street.

He followed it to Glenayr Avenue, crossed over and continued on until he came to the block of flats next to the car wash. It was a typical old Bondi block of red brick flats built in the thirties. Six in the front and six at the back, divided by an entrance and stairs on the right. A narrow driveway ran past the entrance to an uncovered parking area at the rear, and a rickety wooden fence separated the block from the car wash. There were no verandahs, and towels hung from some of the window sills facing the street; pinned across a window on the second floor was a Jamaican flag. Les stood in the driveway and stared up at the flats, wondering which one belonged to Lasjoz and how he was going to time it so he'd be in there when Lasjoz wasn't home. Les was pondering on this when a white Holden station wagon slowly reversed down the driveway towards him. There was a stepladder on top, mops, brooms and other cleaning equipment in the back, and behind the wheel was Gary Jackson. Les stepped aside as the station wagon drew level then tapped on the roof.

'Jacko,' said Les. 'How's things?'

Gary stopped the car and looked up. 'Les. What's happening mate?'

'I'm looking for someone,' replied Les. 'What's your story?'

'I'm the caretaker here.'

'You're the main man,' beamed Les. 'Well, how about that.'

Gary winked. 'You know the old Russian saying, Les. There's no menial jobs. Only menial attitudes.'

'Exactly, Gary,' smiled Les. 'Never swap your backbone for a wish bone. Hey, talking about Russians, Gary. I'm looking for a bloke lives here called Lasjoz. Great big bloke with black hair. You wouldn't know which flat he lives in, would you?'

'That'd be Lurch,' replied Gary. 'He lives in number nine at the back.'

'Lurch. That sounds like him,' said Les.

'That's what I call him anyway. I'll tell you what though,' said Gary, 'he's got to be the strongest cunt I ever seen in me life.'

'Yeah?'

'My oath. I was out the back one day, and I asked him if he'd give me a lift with an old washing machine. Fair dinkum. He didn't say a word. He just picked the fuckin thing up and threw it in the back of the wagon like it was a packet of Sao biscuits.'

'Yeah. That'd be him,' nodded Les. 'And he lives in number nine?'

'Yeah,' nodded Gary. 'He might be home. I'm not sure.'

'Okay,' said Les. 'Thanks, Gary.'

'No worries,' replied Gary. 'Hey, and thanks again for that tip, Les. Shit, we're still counting the money.'

'Any time, mate,' smiled Les. 'Oh, and tell Irish John I went round to that house in Brassie Street. But it was burnt down.'

'Yeah,' said Gary. 'It was a bloody drug lab or something. Strike me hooray. What's Bondi coming to?'

'Yeah. It's got me stuffed,' said Les.

'Mate. I got to go,' said Gary. 'I got a heap of work on today.'

Les stepped aside. 'Go for your life, Gary,' he said. 'Get out there and taste that sweet smell of success.'

'You got it. Either lead, follow or get out of me fuckin road. Hey, what happened to your eye Les?'

'Occupational hazard, Jacko,' smiled Les.

'Say no more. Say no more.' Gary bipped the horn and drove off.

Well, there you go, smiled Les, as he started walking away. Lurch lives in flat nine. I could get my zinger and come back. But I might leave it for the time being. Best I put my Bugs Bunny hat on and do some very heavy concentrationing on this. If Lasjoz can throw a washing machine in the back of a station wagon, if he sprung me in his flat he'd throw me straight out the window. And number nine ain't on the ground floor. Les turned right into Glenayr Avenue and continued home.

Back at Chez Norton, Les placed his phone on the kitchen table and had another glass of water. He was still revved up and bouncing around from all the coffee and wondering what to do with himself. He knew he couldn't do anything strenuous. But he had to do something. I know what I'll do, thought Les. I'll go for another walk in Centennial Park. Les changed back into his old grey tracksuit and was about to leave the house when his mobile rang.

'Hello?'

'Hello my friend,' rasped the voice at the other end.

Norton's eyes narrowed. 'Deep Throat. How are you, mate.'

'I am good.' Suddenly Deep throat sneezed violently. 'Oh. Maybe not so good. Shit.'

'Gesundheit,' said Les cheerfully.

'Yeah. Whatever. So tell me, my friend,' continued Deep Throat. 'How did you go yesterday?'

'At that place in Lamrock Avenue?' said Les.

'Yes. That one. What happened?'

'I found the bag,' said Les.

There was silence at the other end for a moment. 'Say again, please.'

'I found the green bag with the eagle on the side,' lied Les. 'And everything else.'

'You found it?'

'That's right — my friend. And I got you to thank.'

'But. Well, that is good, my friend. Very good. And it was in the house?'

'Sure was,' said Les. 'The front door was unlocked. I walked straight in. And bingo! There it was. Sitting on the lounge. In. Out. Five minutes.'

'That is amazing,' said Deep Throat.

'It sure is,' said Les. 'Now seeing as I'm going to get a reward out of this, I think you and I should meet up, so I can throw a bit your way.'

'No, no. That is quite impossible. I cannot meet you.'

'Why not?' said Les. 'Come on. Let's get together. I want to shake your hand and thank you personally. You sound like a good bloke.'

'No. I am sorry my friend. I cannot do this.' Suddenly Deep Throat sneezed again.

'Yes you can,' said Les. 'Come on. I'm dying to meet you.'

'No. You have the bag,' sniffled Deep Throat. 'Everything is good. Now I must go.'

'No. Don't go,' said Les.

'Goodbye my friend.'

'Hey, don't go. Hello? Hello? You there?' The phone went dead in Norton's hand. 'Fuck you! You dopey fuckin wog cunt!' Les shouted into the phone.

Les clicked off and tossed his phone back on the kitchen table. Bugger it, he fumed. I certainly blew that. I should have strung the prick along a bit more. Too bloody late now. Les drummed his fingers irritably on the table. Shit! I'd love to know who it was. Les calmed down, had a glass of water then locked the house and drove down to Centennial Park.

Ambling along, taking his time and thinking about this and that, Les walked for almost two hours. The sky had clouded over, cooling the afternoon down, so he hardly raised a sweat and it was a leisurely way to spend the end of the day. When he'd finished, Les drove home, had a Promite special sandwich and a cup of tea, then filled the bath and had another soak.

You know, thought Les as he sat in the bath, gingerly shaving away the stubble while he held a hand mirror, life ain't too bad. Okay, I might be a bit battered and bruised. But there's ten thousand bucks sitting in my wardrobe that I didn't have to raise a finger to earn. I got a good sort coming round later with some food. And I don't have to get up and catch a bus to work tomorrow. Besides that, smiled Les, when I dry off and get changed, I'm going to drop some more of those little white pills and things will get better again. I don't know whether Topaz is keen for a root, but I'm not. Imagine if I went for a face full of ted and she ripped all the stitches out. Ouch! Les placed the mirror and razor on the side of the bath and stared out the bathroom window at the darkening sky. Yes. I suppose we have our differences now and again, boss. But all up, we don't get on too bad. Thanks, mate. Les pulled the plug, dabbed on a little Tabac, then dried off, gave his dark blue tracksuit another run and went out to the kitchen.

Norton's two packets of mother's little helpers were still sitting on the table. Les smiled, poured a stiff delicious, and washed down two from each packet. Right, he told himself, rubbing his hands together. I've got about half an hour before I turn into a blancmange. What will I do? Leave the front door ajar, so I don't have to get up off my big fat arse when Topaz gets here and open it. And make sure there's something nice for her to drink. There's enough booze in the bar to supply a cruise liner with Long Island Teas. But I imagine like most women, Topaz would enjoy a glass of chilled white wine. Les checked the back of the fridge and smiled. Warren had left two bottles of Cullen Margaret River Chardonnay behind the meat cabinet. That should suffice admirably, smiled Les. He closed the fridge, half opened the front door then slipped a CD on and settled back to await Topaz's arrival. Down to the Bone were halfway through 'It's A Long Way To Brooklyn' and Les had hit the wall when there was a knock on the front door.

'Yeah. It's open,' Les called out. 'Step right on in.'

The door closed and Les heard footsteps coming down the hallway. Next thing Topaz was standing in the loungeroom wearing a pair of crutch tight black jeans and a lacy grey top under a grey leather jacket. A vapour trail of Chanel No. 5 hung in the air behind her, cleavage was being pushed to its limits and her shining dark hair was swirling round her shoulders like freshly spun silk. Over one shoulder was a red leather handbag and in her other hand she held a large white plastic bag.

Norton's face spread into a beautiful, friendly wide grin. 'Hello Topaz,' he said happily. 'How are you? And might I say, you look absolutely drop-dead gorgeous.'

'I'm good,' said Topaz. She looked at Les a little suspiciously. 'You haven't been smoking dope, have you?'

Les shook his head. 'No. But I was in a lot of pain. So I took some prescription drugs the doctor gave me.'

'Prescription drugs,' said Topaz. 'Like what?'

'Panadeine Forte and Valium,' smiled Les. 'Two of each.'

'Christ! You're going to be a lot of company.'

'No. I'm okay,' grinned Les. 'Just a little — tranquil, that's all.'

'Tranquillised would be more like it.' Topaz held up the white plastic bag. 'I hope you're still hungry.'

'You needn't worry about that,' Les assured her.

'Hey, I like your house,' said Topaz, taking a quick peruse. 'Nice furniture. And those prints are great. Especially that photo of the fish.'

'I took that,' said Les.

'You did?'

'Yeah. I fluked it round the front of Bondi one morning with a disposable camera.' Les finished his delicious and rose unsteadily to his feet. 'Can I get you a drink?'

'Would you have glass of white wine?'

'How about some Cullen Margaret River Chardonnay?'

'Well,' flustered Topaz. 'If you haven't got anything else, I suppose that will just have to do. Won't it?'

They went into the kitchen and Topaz placed the food on the table. After a couple of attempts, Les was able to open a bottle of wine and pour Topaz a glass. He made himself another delicious, then they talked about different things while Les managed to bumble around and get in the way as Topaz organised some plates and warmed the container of chicken soup in the microwave. Topaz didn't mind a cool one and the best part of a bottle was gone when they got down to eating.

'Ohh, stop the fight,' said Les after two mouthfuls. 'This soup is unbelievable. And it's almost like a casserole.'

'Yes, Mum does a good job,' agreed Topaz. 'She adds a little prosciutto ham. Red and green lentils. A little mustard oil. You know what those old wog sheilas are like.'

'Yeah. They sure got the old "je ne sais quoi" haven't they,' said Les.

Out of it or not, Les ripped in. Topaz had even brought a loaf of crispy white bread which Les used to wipe the bowl clean. Next came the rhubarb and banana pie. Topaz warmed it up in the microwave and they had it with scoops of ice cream. The homemade pie brought Les to his knees.

'Ohh how good's this?' crooned Les. 'I've never tasted anything like it.'

'Yes. It's got a bitter sweetness about it,' said Topaz. 'The rhubarb complements the banana.'

'It hits the bloody spot, I know that,' said Les.

They finished eating. Les said don't worry about the dishes, he'd do them in the morning. This suited Topaz and Les opened the other bottle of Margaret River. He poured himself another delicious and offered Topaz some Valium, but she declined.

'All right,' smiled Les. 'What will we do now? Watch a DVD? I got a stack of them there. Warren brings them home from work by the trunk load.'

'No. I brought one with me,' said Topaz. 'I'm going to see just how much of a tough guy you are.'

'It's not *Million Dollar Baby*, is it?' demanded Les.

'No. *Very Annie Mary*. With Rachel Griffiths.'

'Ohh cool,' said Les. 'She was great in *Muriel's Wedding*. You're terrible, Muriel,' he joked.

'Well, let's see how you handle Rachel Griffiths with a Welsh accent.' Topaz took the DVD from her bag and slipped it into Norton's player and they settled back on the lounge with their drinks.

If *The 300* was one of the worst movies Les had ever seen, *Very Annie Mary* was one of the best. Rachel Griffiths was sensational as the poor simple Welsh girl with the hidden talent, who manages to stuff everything up. Jonathan Pryce was horrible as her overbearing, would-be Pavarotti father. The Village People tribute was a crack-up. And the biggest surprise was Ioan Gruffudd — Captain Horatio Hornblower — turning up as a gay confectionery shop owner. But for all the laughs Les got, the movie also tore his heart out. When it finished, Les was sitting on the lounge mellowed out on Valium, his body racked with sobs and tears pouring down his cheeks.

'Well, I'll be buggered,' smiled Topaz. 'Barbara was right. You are a big softie.'

'I am not a big softie,' wailed Les. 'Oh all right then,' he howled. 'I am a big softie. But what do you bloody expect? Her bloody best friend's got cancer. Her bloody father's a bastard. It bloody turns out she can sing like a bloody nightingale. She pulls up outside the house in the van with the bloody speakers. And when they're doing up the bloody house, they're playing that bloody Fleetwood Mac song. Owhh, ahh wooo,' Les blubbered, and blew his nose on a tissue. 'Why did it have to have such a happy ending? I feel awful.'

'All right, settle down, Les,' said Topaz. 'It's okay. It's only a movie.'

'Settle down,' sniffed Les, noticing Topaz was still dry-eyed. 'You must have a heart of bloody stone if you didn't cry at that.'

'Les,' said Topaz. 'I've seen it five times.'

'You have?'

'Yes. It's one of my favourites.'

'Well, all right then,' sniffed Les.

'Ohh come here, you poor baby.'

Topaz cuddled Les to her bosom and gave him a gentle kiss. Les kissed her back and the kiss went on a bit. Topaz had lovely soft lips and she kissed beautifully. But it hurt Norton's swollen mouth like he couldn't believe. Topaz sensed Les wincing and drew back.

'Does your mouth hurt, Les?' she asked.

'Yeah. A bit, Topaz,' admitted Les.

'How are you feeling after all that Valium?'

'Pretty good,' shrugged Les. 'Why?'

Topaz ground herself up to Norton. 'Well, all that wine's made me as horny as buggery. I'd like a little sex.'

'Shit,' replied Les. 'So would I, I suppose. But Valium ain't actually Viagra. And my face and head is full of stitches. If I rip the stitches, my doctor will kill me.'

'That's all right,' smiled Topaz. 'You can lay back and I can get on top.'

'Yeah?' said Les.

'Yes,' nodded Topaz. 'But there's just one other thing.'

'Yeah. What's that? A condom? No worries.'

'No,' said Topaz. 'It's your face. All those bruises and black eyes. And stitches and bandages. It looks horrible.'

'Well, there's not much I can do about it,' said Les.

'Yes there is,' replied Topaz.

'Like what?'

'How about putting a bag over your head?'

Les drew back and stared at Topaz in disbelief. 'Would you care to repeat that, please?'

'I said, how about putting a bag over your head?' repeated Topaz.

'You actually want to bonk me with a bag over my head?'

'Yes,' nodded Topaz. 'What's wrong with that?'

Trying to maintain his pride. Les took in a deep breath and gave Topaz an indignant once up and down. 'Topaz,' Les said, deliberately, 'what would you do, if you were a bit on the ugly side, and I called round to your place, got half full of drink, then said, I'd like a root, but stick a bag over your head first?'

'I'd tell you to get fucked and boot your arse out the door, you male chauvinist pig,' replied Topaz. 'What sort of a moll do you take me for?'

'Exactly,' said Les.

'So what's your answer?' said Topaz, taking an insouciant sip of her wine. 'Yes or no?'

Les took a deep breath then exhaled. 'Did you bring a bag with you?'

'I certainly did,' smiled Topaz. She reached into the white plastic bag and took out a brown paper Telstra bag with two handles on it. 'Look,' she said. 'I even cut two little eye holes in it for your eyes. And one for your mouth.'

'Very considerate of you,' said Les. 'Okay. My bedroom's at the front. Let's go. And if anybody finds out about this, Topaz, you'll never drink Margaret River Chardonnay in this house again.'

Topaz gave Les a quick, soft kiss. 'You don't really mean that.'

They got up and walked down to Norton's bedroom where they got undressed. Les was a bit clumsy. But in no time Topaz was standing in the light from Norton's bed lamp with nothing covering her voluptuous body but a lacy black G-string.

Mr Wobbly was quick to notice this and, full of Valium or not, he soon rose angrily to the occasion, demanding in on the action. Les found a condom in his drawer, cracked it open and was just about to slip it on when Topaz eased him down on the bed, smiled and gave Les a brain-snapping polish that sent Mr Wobbly into a drug affected frenzy. Topaz finished and slipped off her G-string, Les slipped the condom onto Mr Wobbly and Topaz slipped the bag over Norton's head.

'Jesus, I feel like a nice dill,' mumbled Les, from behind the hole Topaz had cut out for his mouth.

'Don't worry about it,' smiled Topaz. 'You got a hot body.' She adjusted the pillow beneath Norton's head, then got on the bed and straddled him.

It might have been the weirdest sex Les had ever had, but it still felt good. Topaz was tight and moist and Mr Wobbly's nasty little head had swelled up like a big red Fuji apple. Topaz started off in first gear then slipped into second before she hit high gear and flattened it, making sure Norton's neighbours on both sides knew what a good time she was having. Les lay back comfortably and through the holes in the paper bag, got a tunnelled vision of Topaz's raptuous facial expressions framed by her beautiful dark hair swirling from side to side. Les would loved to have kissed her. But he was content to reach up and feel the firmness of her body and breasts and softly massage her rock-hard nipples with his fingers.

The Valium and painkillers had slowed down Norton's libido, so Topaz certainly got her money's worth. But after a while Mr Wobbly could take no more and he exploded beneath the condom nearly blowing it to shreds. Topaz gave one long scream then settled down. After a few minutes they both got their breath back.

'How are you feeling, Les?' crooned Topaz.

'Pretty good, thanks Topaz,' replied Les. 'Is it okay if I take the bag off now?'

'Sure. And thanks for that, Les. It made all the difference.'

'Anything to oblige, ma'am.' Les took the bag off his head and tossed it down the side of the bed with the condom inside. 'Give me a minute,' he said, woozily, 'and I'll organise a taxi for you. Would you like a cup of coffee or something first?'

'No. That's all right,' replied Topaz. 'But stay there. I can ring.'

'Righto,' said Les.

Les pulled the duvet over himself and had a perv on Topaz while she got dressed. When she was fully clothed, she went to the kitchen and returned shortly with her two bags.

'I turned off the lights,' she said. 'And I souvenired the rest of that Margaret River for a nightcap. Is that okay?'

'Sure. Help yourself,' said Les.

Topaz sat on the edge of the bed. 'That was fun, Les. I really enjoyed it. I'd like to get with you again, when your face is all right and you're not full of Valium. I reckon you'd be a tiger.'

'On a good night, with the right moon and tide, I'm not bad,' smiled Les. 'I give it everything I got.'

'I'm sure you do.' A horn tooted out the front. 'There's the taxi. All you have to do now is go to sleep.' Topaz kissed Les on the lips. 'Goodnight, Les,' she smiled. 'I'll give you a ring.'

'Goodnight Topaz. And thanks for coming over. It was really nice of you.'

Topaz turned off Norton's bedroom lights and disappeared out the front door, leaving Les in darkness. Well, I don't know what to make of that, mused Les as he heard the taxi drive off. I degraded myself and sunk about as low as any man can go. But shit a brick! It was still a pretty good root. Les smiled and sprawled back happily into the pillows. The smile was still etched on his face well after he fell asleep.

Looking at himself in the bathroom mirror the next morning, Les could certainly understand why Topaz asked him to put a bag over his head. And although there was a funny side to it, Les didn't think he'd be telling too many people what happened. After finishing in the bathroom, Les walked out to the kitchen, put the kettle on and got some scrambled eggs together. He was late rising and after a solid night's sleep, apart from the initial stiffness, he was feeling good. He would have liked a run or a good hit out on the bag. But Les knew he'd only tear the stitches; it was only through luck and Topaz's audacity he didn't tear any the night before. Les decided he'd go for another good long walk. After cleaning up, he changed into his old grey tracksuit, got his sunglasses and baseball cap and drove down to Centennial Park.

Les wasn't the only person out enjoying the morning. There was no shortage of joggers and walkers and pods of bike riders. Some people walked or jogged past that he knew from around Bondi. But they didn't recognise him behind his sunglasses with his cap pulled down, so Les didn't have to stop and talk and answer any stupid questions about his appearance. While he was strolling along Les pondered what he was going to do about Bodene's script. Today was as good a day as any to have a look in Lasjoz's flat and see if it was in there. If not, knock the whole idea on the head. Tarot cards or no tarot cards. But for the sake of a lazy fifty falling in, it was worth one last throw of the dice. Getting into Lasjoz's flat was no problem. But how was he going to make sure the monster wasn't there? By the time Les finished walking, he'd cooked up half an idea.

Back at Chez Norton, Les had a shower, then changed into his black cargoes, clean trainers and a white Margaritaville T-shirt he bought in Florida. He was standing in the kitchen drinking water when the phone rang in the loungeroom.

'Hello?'

'Hello Les. It's Marla.'

'Hey, Marla,' smiled Les. 'How are you?'

'Real good,' came the bubbly voice at the other end. 'How's yourself?'

'Always better when I hear from you, Marla. You know why?'

'Why?'

'Because your voice is the rain that makes the flowers bloom in the garden of my heart.'

'Oh Les, you're so sweet.'

'I know. Mum told me never to go outside when it's raining because sugar melts when it's wet. So what's doing, mate?'

'Well,' said Marla. 'There's been somewhat of a new development up here.'

'There has?' enquired Les.

'Yes. My ex-boyfriend Milton got busted with two ounces of coke.'

'Two ounces? Ohh lucky boy,' said Les. 'That entitles him to a free holiday. No problem at all.'

'I know. He's started already,' chuckled Marla. 'The court wouldn't grant him bail.'

'Yes. They're funny like that with coke dealers.'

'I always suspected Milton was using. But I didn't know he was dealing.'

'Didn't he have the local cops on side or something?' asked Les. 'They were keen to bust my arse, I know that.'

'These cops were from Newcastle,' said Marla. 'They arrived with a sniffer dog and everything.'

'Fair dinkum?'

'Anyway. When they were going through Milton's house, the dog's gone into Barry's room — the bloke you punched out — and they found fifty deals of ice. And a gun.'

'Even better,' laughed Les. 'The family gets to go on holiday.'

'So those two cops looking for you have dropped Barry like a hot potato. He can forget the assault charges. All Barry's got to look forward to when he gets out of hospital is going to gaol. Along with Milton.'

'And a big fat lawyer's bill. So who told you all this?' Les asked.

'My friend in the council,' replied Marla. 'But not only that. Hickey, the one that threatened he was going to get you.'

'The dill with the nutty family,' said Les. 'What's he done?'

'They were coming back from the Bateau Bay Hotel drunk on Wednesday night, and Hickey rolled the car. They're all in hospital. Hickey's got two broken legs.'

'Ohh, what a shame,' said Les. 'Let me know which hospital he's in and I'll make sure he gets some flowers and chocolates.'

'I'm sure you will,' laughed Marla. 'So it looks like your guardian angel's been working overtime, Les. And you can come back up here any time you like.'

Les looked at his battered face in the mirror above the bar. 'My guardian angel, eh,' he chuckled. 'But that's good, Marla. It's made my day.'

'I thought you'd like it. Anyway. I'm at work, Les. And it's piling up again. How about ringing me at home tonight? And you can tell me when you're coming back to see me.'

'Okay Marla. I'll ring you tonight,' said Les. 'Thanks for the call.'

'Bye.'

Les hung up and smiled at the phone. I don't know about guardian angels, Marla, he mused. I think with those dills it's more like, you get what's coming to you. Still, you never know. As for me coming back to see you? I'd love to. But I'd better get the stitches out first. Now, where was I? Oh yes. Operation Lasjoz.

Les went back to his glass of water in the kitchen. While he'd been walking earlier, Les remembered seeing one of Gary Jackson's mates working at the car wash when he'd been perusing Lasjoz's block of flats the day before. A tall skinny bloke with untidy dark hair. Chamois Davis, Jnr.

Chamois's real name was Marshall Davis, Jnr. His father, Marshall Davis, Snr, had been a fairly famous golfer and named his son after him. Marshall never rose to any great heights and was content to hang round the beach and work at the car wash. Marshall came down the hotel one night trying to sell his friends some chamois leathers he'd nicked from work and a drunk nicknamed him Chamois Davis, Jnr. Which got shortened to Chamois Davis then plain old Chamois. Chamois was always on the hustle for a dollar and Norton felt he might be the answer to his problem. Les finished his glass of water, got the zinger from his bedroom, put his cap and sunglasses on and left for the car wash.

There was the usual bustle of people in Hall Street and no shortage of punters seated in the sun around the local coffee shops. Les was tempted to stop for a quick caffeine fix, but kept on down Glenayr Avenue. As he turned left at Curlewis Street, he noticed Bodene and his friends in the distance seated outside Azulejos and the council still digging up the road with what appeared to be a few extra council workers standing around, busting their arses trying to avoid doing any work. He couldn't see Lasjoz. But Topaz and Barbara were seated under the trees with Bodene and the same three men as the day before, and the coffee shop was doing a brisk trade. Les strode past the old block of flats and straight into the Curlewis Car Wash, situated next door, on the left-hand side of the service station.

It was a typical car wash. Huge roller brushes, water jets, long plastic flaps hanging down, big vacuum cleaners. Outside was a smattering of chairs and tables where the customers could sit and have a coffee or whatever while they waited for their car to be cleaned. Business was quiet and two men were Squeegeeing water from the driveway while Chamois was seated at one of the tables in a pair of black shorts, a black T-shirt and gum boots, sucking on a cigarette. He looked up as Les approached.

'Hello Chamois,' smiled Norton. 'How's things, mate?'

'Les,' replied Chamois. 'How are you, mate?' Chamois had a quick glance around. 'Where's your car?'

'Home.'

'Oh?'

'So what are you doing, Chamois?' asked Les. 'Taking a breather?'

'Reckon,' replied Chamois sincerely. 'I've been working me ring off all morning. This is the first break I've had.'

'How would you like to earn fifty bucks for five minutes' work?'

Chamois gave Les a suspicious once up and down. 'Fifty bucks for five minutes' work. What've I got to do, Les? Help you get rid of a body? Give you a lift with a crate of machine guns? Long Bay doesn't appeal to me that much, Les. I'm quite happy to plug along here, workin' at the car wash, baby. Just like in the song.'

Les shook his head. 'Jesus, you've got a low opinion of me, Chamois. No.' Les pointed to the block of flats. 'All I want you to do, is go up to that block of flats, knock on number nine and see if there's anybody home. If a big bloke answers the door, just say

207

you're looking for Charlie Brown or whoever. Then tell him you've got the wrong address and leave.'

'Fifty bucks?' said Chamois.

'That's right,' answered Les. 'I just want to know if this bloke's home. That's all.'

Chamois stared at Norton for a quick second then butted his cigarette. 'Righto. Wait here.'

Les pulled up a seat and made himself comfortable as Chamois disappeared into the block of flats. Before long Chamois was on his way back. He walked up to Les and shrugged.

'No one home,' said Chamois.

'Are you sure?' Les asked. 'How many times did you knock?'

'Three times. Loud enough to raise the dead.'

'Okay.' Les stood up and handed Chamois two fifties. 'There's another fifty for luck.'

'Shit! Thanks, Les,' said Chamois, pocketing the money. 'Hey. If you need me again. Just give me a yell.'

'Righto, Chamois. I will.' Les exited the car wash and stepped inside the entrance to the block of flats.

Number nine was on the second floor. There was no dust or rubbish on the stairs going up, Jacko did a good job as a caretaker, and the walls and windows had been wiped clean of any scuff marks or dirt. Les arrived on the landing and stepped over to a wooden veneer door next to a disused servery. He knocked on the door a couple of times to be sure, then took out his zinger. A few seconds later Les was inside. He removed his sunglasses and had a look around.

Lasjoz's flat wasn't very big. A kitchen on the left ran off a short hallway that led into the loungeroom, the bathroom was in the corner on the right and a bedroom was behind the loungeroom on the left. Furnishings were sparse. But the flat was very tidy. A black leather lounge sitting on a blue weave carpet faced a flat-screen TV and a small stereo. Against a wall on the left was a cabinet half full of CDs and DVDs; against the opposite wall was a solid wooden table, two chairs and a computer. Coloured bottles, vases and other bric-a-brac sat along the cornices and several travel posters of lakes and mountain scenes in Albania hung on the walls. Everything was neat and tidy and had a freshness about it that gave Les the impression Lasjoz hadn't been living there long. Anyway, thought Les, I didn't come here to do a spread for *Home Beautiful*. The sooner I do my shifty business and blast off, the better. I don't even want to think what would happen if Lasjoz found me in here. I'll start with the lounge.

Les carefully went through the drawers in the CD and DVD cabinet first and found nothing, except that Lasjoz's musical tastes were very middle of the road, ranging from Neil Diamond to the Beatles, and he was a Clint Eastwood fan. There was another set of drawers under the window and one next to the computer table. They revealed nothing either. Righto, thought Les, I'll try the bedroom.

The bedroom contained a king-size bed with a black and white duvet, a dressing table and mirror and a solid wardrobe with a mirror on the front very similar to the one Les had in his bedroom. Carefully again, Les went through the drawers on the dressing table. There was no green bag. But Lasjoz kept his T-shirts, sox, Reg Grundys and hankies folded tidily and neatly separated from each other. As he was going through the drawers, Les noticed every T-shirt was size XXXL and a few beads of nervous sweat formed on his forehead. He looked at his watch and moved across to the wardrobe.

There was plenty of light coming from the window above the dressing table, Les opened the wardrobe and peered inside. Hanging up were two dark-coloured suits, several shirts, two leather jackets and a grey check sports coat. All Lasjoz needs, smiled Les, is a few Hawaiian shirts and an East German Navy jacket and this could almost be my wardrobe. Suddenly the ACME Pty Ltd, Wile E. Coyote light bulb lit up above Norton's head. Oooh. What's that you say, Shintaro? Les asked himself. My wardrobe? I wonder? I just fuckin wonder? Les tapped on the rear of the wardrobe and sure enough, it had a hollow section. He ran his hand along the bottom of the panel and poking out of the wood was the end of a self-tapping screw. Well, what do you know, smiled Les. Great minds do think alike. Les pushed the screw to the left and the panel slid open.

Inside was a plastic bag full of fifties which, at a rough guess, Les estimated to be five thousand dollars. There was another, smaller, locktop plastic bag full of pills, which could have been anything from LSD to ecstasy. And stuffed down the back was a green leather handbag with a bronze clasp on top and a black eagle on the side.

'Well, well, well,' said Les. 'What have we here?'

Les put everything else back and closed the panel, then took the green bag out into the loungeroom and unzipped it. Inside was a plastic bound film script with *The Case Of The Talking Pie Crust*, copyright Post No Gravy Productions Pty Ltd, Australia, on the front. A floppy disc. Another copy of the synopsis for *Gone With the Willy Willy*. And three small hardcover books of old cartoons by Emile Mercier called *Gravy Pie, Sauce or Mustard*, and *My Wife's Swallowed a Bishop*.

'What I have here in my hands,' grinned Les, 'is a new hybrid car. Thank you, Lasjoz. And thank you, Bodene Menjou.'

Les put everything back in the bag and zipped it up. He was about to leave when there was the sound of heavy footsteps on the landing before the door opened and Lasjoz stepped into the flat wearing a white T-shirt tucked into a pair of jeans with a short-sleeved blue shirt hanging out over the top. He closed the door behind him then his face clouded over when he turned around and noticed Les standing in the loungeroom.

'Les Norton,' he growled. 'What you are doing in my flat?'

'What I am doing in your flat, Lasjoz?' swallowed Les. He held up the green bag. 'Looking for this.'

Lasjoz's eyes narrowed. 'So,' he said. 'You find bag.'

'Yes. I find bag,' said Les.

'How you find bag?'

'Because I'm clever, Lasjoz,' replied Les.

A crooked, mirthless smile appeared on Lasjoz's jowly face. 'Maybe too fucking clever for your own fucking good, Les Norton.'

'Now hold on a second, Lasjoz,' said Les. 'You don't have to be like that. There's no reason we can't work something out here.'

'Work something out. What?'

'I'll tell Bodene I found the bag somewhere else,' suggested Les. 'And you and I can split the reward money. Sixty-forty your way.'

'Split fucking money,' exclaimed Lasjoz. 'Why you think I stole bag in first place? So I can share fucking money?'

'Well, no. But why did you steal the bag?' asked Les, figuring while he was talking, Lasjoz wasn't trying to choke him and he could work out an escape.

'For fucking money. Why you think?' shouted Lasjoz. 'Bodene pay me shit.' The big man indicated round his flat. 'Look what I live.'

'I don't know,' said Les. 'I've seen worse.'

'Where? Fucking Bangladesh.'

'Jamaica?'

'Pah!' Lasjoz spat on the carpet. 'So how come you know I steal bag?'

'You shouldn't have used one of your gay pals as a go-between,' said Les. 'Bodene picked up on his voice. And shit. Even I know you're gay.'

'How you know I am gay?' demanded Lasjoz.

'Your clothes.'

'My clothes?'

'Yeah. And the way you walk,' answered Les. 'You want to learn to take bigger steps.'

Lasjoz banged his huge fist against the wall. 'Enough of this fucking bullshit,' he thundered. 'Now you die, Les Norton. Clever, stupid bastard. Then I cut you up. And take you for swim with sharks.' Lasjoz advanced towards Les with his huge hands open and a horrible smile on his face. 'How you want die, Mr Clever? Easy? Or hard?'

Les stared grimly at Lasjoz for a second. 'Hard,' said Les. 'Real fuckin hard.' Saying that, Les hurled the green bag at Lasjoz's head.

The bag hit Lasjoz in the face and only made him blink angrily. Les stepped forward and belted the big man with a straight left and a right cross. It was like punching a bag of cement. Lasjoz rocked on his feet for a second, then spat a little blood from a split lip and smiled.

'Stupid little man,' he said, then swung his massive right arm round and backhanded Les across the face.

The force sent Norton's cap flying and knocked him over the lounge before he landed on his back, seeing stars. He shook his head and started getting to get to his feet when Lasjoz reached down, grabbed him by the front of his T-shirt, and hurled him across the other side of the room. Les managed to cover his head before he crashed into the computer table, sending the computer one way and anything else on the table the other. Les sucked in some air before Lasjoz took him by the scruff of his T-shirt and flung him back over the lounge. Les covered up again and barrelled noisily into the CD cabinet scattering CDs and DVDs everywhere. Les got up and shook his head, then set himself and kicked the advancing Lasjoz in the groin and punched him in the face with two sizzling left hooks. Norton's heart sunk as Lasjoz stopped and smiled at him.

'Is that best you got?' sneered Lasjoz. 'And you call me poofter.'

Lasjoz grabbed Les by the front of his T-shirt with one hand and the front of his cargoes with the other, lifted Les up and flung him over his head across the room. Les covered up and yelped as he sailed over the lounge and crashed back onto the computer table, smashing it beneath him before landing on the floor amongst the wreckage.

'Ohh fuck!' winced Les, holding his ribs.

Lasjoz laughed menacingly. 'Funny you should say fuck, Les Norton. Because that is what I do before I kill you. And you like my fuck. Guarantee. But before this,' said Lasjoz, looking down on Les. 'I have fun. Like cat with little mouse.'

Ripping the neck open, Lasjoz grabbed Les by his T-shirt and hurled him back across the room into what was left of the CD cabinet. Les barely had time to glimpse the stars spinning round in front of him before he felt himself being flung across the room again into the TV set, sending it and the stereo crashing onto the floor. Les gulped in some air as Lasjoz grabbed him by a leg, flung him against the lounge, then threw him across the room into the wall opposite the wrecked computer table.

'Hey. How you like so far, little man,' laughed Lasjoz. 'Is good? Well, don't worry.' The monster rubbed his groin. 'Best is yet to come.'

Les looked up at Lasjoz laughing at him from across the other side of the room and the beads of nervous sweat he felt earlier when he was searching the big man's bedroom were now streaming down his face. Norton knew if he didn't do something, and quick, he was gone. Rose the tarot lady warned him the time might come when he would have to dig deep. She was right. Without a knife or a gun, there was only one way he could stop Lasjoz. Les was going to have to use the fearsome Mongolian Death Lock.

Les learnt the Mongolian Death Lock by sheer chance after school one day in Dirranbandi. Of all the people in the world, a family of Mongolians stopped at Dirranbandi for two weeks on a cultural exchange. They had two sons, Hatgal and Halvan, who attended the local school to mix with the kids and learn a little about Australian education. Although Hatgal and Halvan's English was limited, Les and his brother Murray befriended them and liked the strange clothes they wore, especially their pointy-toed boots. But kids are kids. And fat Buddha Bailey, the school bully, wanted to fight the Mongolian kids, who weren't at all interested. Young Les and Murray were walking home from school one afternoon with the Mongolian kids when Buddha Bailey appeared on the scene and started shoving Hatgal around. Before Les and Murray had a chance to intervene, Buddha was lying on his back gasping for breath and they thought he was going to die. Buddha never knew what hit him and Les and Murray weren't sure either. But they asked Hatgal to show them what he did. Hatgal reluctantly agreed, but warned Les and

Murray only to ever use the death lock as a last resort. Because as well as being unbreakable, it was deadly. And even if you were strong enough to break it, you only had seconds to do so before you either blacked out or died.

Through his sweat, pain and ripped clothing, Les blinked up at the leering Lasjoz. He didn't particularly want to kill him and go through a great hassle with the police. But if he could apply the grip just long enough, he could get away, take the script to Bodene and spill the beans on Lasjoz, who would no doubt get a bullet or three in the head from his boss. Les half rose to his feet as Lasjoz swept the lounge aside and came slowly and confidently towards him.

'Now little man,' Lasjoz scoffed from behind the sinister smile on his face, 'I think I put your head down shithouse. Drown you little bit like rat. Then fuck you. Before I slit your throat.'

Les flicked the huge Albanian a thin smile. 'Lasjoz,' he said, evenly. 'You wouldn't have a dick big enough, or a knife that sharp.'

Les waited till Lasjoz was almost on top him, then leapt to his feet and with all the strength left in his body, hit Lasjoz in the heart with a perfectly timed left rip. It wasn't enough to flatten the giant. But it made him grunt with pain, shut his eyes and stop for a moment. This was all the time Les needed to quickly step behind Lasjoz and kick his legs away. As Lasjoz fell back against him, Les slipped his right arm around the big man's throat, jammed the edge of his wrist against Lasjoz's Adam's Apple then closed his right fist and gripping it tight with his left hand, pulled the big man back down to the floor. When he landed on his rump, Les jammed his right knee into the nape of Lasjoz's huge neck then sat back and started crushing Lasjoz's throat between his right knee and his wrist.

With the oxygen supply to his brain completely cut off, Lasjoz gagged and coughed and tried frantically to tear Norton's arms away. But to no avail. Les kept squeezing Lasjoz's throat in a vice-like grip till the big man's eyes began to burst. The seconds ticked by and Lasjoz's kicking and flailing attempts to free himself got weaker and weaker before they finally stopped and he slumped unconscious in Norton's arms. Les held the Mongolian Death Lock for another second or two, then released it and stood up to get his breath back.

Lying on his back at Norton's feet, Lasjoz's bloodshot eyes were bulging out of his head, his face was dark blue and his tongue was protuding through a pair of blackened lips. Les was sure he'd killed him, when a ghastly rattling sound escaped Lasjoz's mouth and he managed to suck a little air into his lungs. Les stepped across and kicked him in the balls several times with the heel of his trainer in case he looked like getting up. The only movement from Lasjoz was another tortured gasp of air and a feeble attempt to place his hand against his ruptured throat.

Les stood back and smiled down at Lasjoz. 'Well Lasjoz,' he said. 'I hate to tell you this old mate, but from where I'm standing, I'd say you're the one that just got fucked.'

Les tucked what was left of his T-shirt in and glanced around the flat. There was broken furniture and other wreckage strewn everywhere. The only things that survived were the lounge and two Albanian travel posters. Les limped into Lasjoz's bedroom to check himself out in the wardrobe mirror and couldn't believe what he saw. His T-shirt was torn and there was a red mark where Lasjoz had backhanded him. And there was no doubt he was going to wake up with a shitload of bruising the next day. But apart from that, he didn't have a mark on him. Not even a stitch got broken.

'Well, how about that,' smiled Les. 'Hey. While my luck's in.'

Les opened the wardrobe, reached down and pulled the panel back and took out the packet of money. After pocketing the plastic bag, Les shut the panel then closed the wardrobe and returned to the loungeroom.

Lasjoz hadn't moved and was still lying on the floor barely breathing. Les gave him another kick in the balls for good luck then picked up his cap along with the green bag from where it fell after he flung it in Lasjoz's face. The zinger was still in his pocket, but Les didn't have a clue where his sunglasses were and didn't particularly care. He had a last look at Lasjoz then moved towards the door.

'Adios Lasjoz, me old China,' saluted Les. 'Don't bother getting up. I can find my own way out.' Les opened the door then stepped out onto the landing, closing it quietly behind him.

Two old ladies in cotton dresses and cardigans were standing on the landing, along with a young blonde woman in jeans and a grey sweat shirt holding a baby.

'What was all the noise in there?' asked one of the old ladies.

'Oh, I'm so sorry about that,' replied Les. 'I was just helping my friend move a piano inside.'

'A piano?' said the other old lady.

'Yes,' smiled Les. 'Back in Poland, Igor was a classical pianist. Didn't you know?'

'No. I didn't,' said the first old lady.

'He sure is,' beamed Les, heading for the stairs. 'As soon as he gets it tuned properly, you'll be able to listen to all your beautiful old favourites. Chopin. Mozart. Beethoven. Rolf Harris.'

'Oh, how lovely,' said the second old lady.

'Yes,' agreed the first old lady. 'Much better than that horrible music they play today.'

'I couldn't agree with you more,' smiled Les. 'Goodbye ladies. Sorry about the noise.'

'That's quite all right. Goodbye, young man.'

Les put his cap on then exited the block of flats and walked towards Glenayr Avenue. Right, determined Les. The sooner I get this bag to Bodene, the sooner I can get my money. And the sooner he can put a bullet in Lasjoz's brain. Christ! I'd hate to have to go through that again. Les got to the corner to wait for the lights to cross over and noticed the other people waiting for the lights were staring grim-faced down Glenayr Avenue. When Les joined them he couldn't believe his eyes. Seven Ways was total pandemonium.

Police and police cars were everywhere. Bodene was against one police car in handcuffs along with one of his friends. Topaz and Barbara were both handcuffed, and what looked like Bodene's two other friends were lying on the grass with black plastic sheets over them. The crowd at Azulejos was standing back with stunned looks on their faces. Two cops were running out yellow Crime Scene tape. The council workers had all downed tools and the loafing council workers Les had noticed earlier were walking around, guns in one hand and walkie-talkies in the other.

'What the fuck?'

Suddenly, Les heard a voice behind him.

'Hello Les.'

Les turned around. It was Detective Maroney wearing the same blue suit as the day before and his sunglasses.

'Rod,' said Les. 'What . . . what's going on?'

Detective Maroney pointed to the green bag and smiled. 'I see you found the green bag with the eagle on the side, Les. Clever little devil, aren't you.'

Les looked at the bag then turned to Detective Maroney, stunned. 'How the fuck . . .?

'Les. Come here.' Detective Maroney moved Les back from the people on the corner. 'What do you think I told you to keep away from Bodene Menjou for? He's been parked outside Azulejos for the last three weeks organising a shipment of coke. It's all up at the pizza shop. Topaz Delimara's the tester. And Barbara Lewis is in on the distribution.'

'You're kiddin,' said Les.

Detective Maroney shook his head. 'The smartie thought all the noise from the council workers would stuff up the surveillance equipment. And he was half right. But we planted sensors all round that little park. And got every word.'

'Every word?' said Les.

'Every word,' nodded Detective Maroney. 'You're on tape,' he smiled. 'In fact the boys got a bit of a laugh about your views on political correctness.'

'Oh shit,' groaned Les.

'It looks like you found the bag all right, Les,' said Detective Maroney. 'But you're going to be a long time waiting for your money. At least twenty-five years.'

'Oh shit,' Les groaned again. 'Shit. Shit. Shit.'

'Something like that, Les. Yeah.'

Les shook his head then looked seriously at Detective Maroney. 'Look, thanks for telling me what you did, Rod. I appreciate it and I had no intention of going near those pricks. But I have to admit, when I found the bag, I was on my way down there to see about my money.'

'That's okay, Les,' said Detective Maroney. 'I don't blame you.'

'So what are you doing up here, Rod? How come you're not down there in the thick of it, guns blazing and the rest of it? Looks like they plugged a couple of them too.'

'They sure did,' nodded Detective Maroney. 'No. I'm just waiting here for back-up and we're going round to arrest the big bloke. Lasjoz Malicnisc. He managed to slip through the cracks. He only lives down the road a bit.'

'Yeah. Next to the car wash,' nodded Les. 'Flat nine.'

'Oh. You're a regular fountain of information, aren't you, Les,' said Detective Maroney.

'I just been round there,' said Les. 'Lasjoz had the bag.'

'What?'

'Rod, I'm going to level with you,' said Les.

Les told Detective Maroney pretty much what happened. He had an idea Lasjoz had the bag, he broke into the flat with a piece of perspex, Lasjoz caught him, they had a fight and Les was lucky enough to choke him out.

Detective Maroney was astounded. 'You choked that big monster out? You must be fuckin Superman.'

'Not really,' replied Les. 'But if you go round there and kick the door in, I reckon you'll still find him lying on the floor. And if you look in a panel in the back of his wardrobe where I found the green bag, you'll find a plastic bag full of pills. You can nick him for those, too.'

'A plastic bag full of pills?' said Detective Maroney. 'And you left them there?'

'Of course I did,' replied Les. 'I didn't want the fuckin things.'

Detective Maroney was impressed. 'Good for you, Les.'

Two police cars pulled up on the corner with four beefy detectives in each vehicle. Les looked at them for a second then turned back to Rod.

'Rod. Do you want to do me a favour?' Les asked.

'It all depends, Les,' answered Detective Maroney. 'What is it?'

'Do you mind if I go home, run a hot bath, put a Neil Young CD on and slash both my wrists. Then come down tomorrow morning and make a statement?'

Detective Maroney thought for a moment. 'Yeah, go on, Les.

Everything's sweet. I'll see you tomorrow and we'll have a coffee or something.'

'Thanks Rod. See you in the morning.' Les watched Detective Maroney get in the first police car and drive off, then turned and, without giving the scene at Seven Ways a second look, started walking back up Glenayr Avenue towards home.

Back at Chez Norton Les placed the green bag on the coffee table in the loungeroom, then put the zinger back in his bedroom and counted the money he stole from Lasjoz. Three thousand, five hundred dollars. Better than a poke in the eye with a Phillips head screwdriver, I suppose, figured Les. He tossed the money in a drawer and, without bothering to get changed, went back to the loungeroom and poured himself a large Vincent Van Gogh Dutch Chocolate Vodka and mineral water and sat down on the lounge. He took a swallow, then another and stared at the green bag. Well, here we are again, smiled Les. More green bags full of goodies. Let's have another look at what I got my head bashed in and almost got myself killed for. Les opened the bag.

The script he wasn't interested in. Nor was he interested in the floppy disc, and he'd already read the synopsis. He looked at one of the little books of cartoons titled *My Wife's Swallowed a Bishop*. On the cover was a man and his wife with a chess board between them. The man was on the phone obviously ringing a doctor and his wife was clutching her throat. Next to her a scraggle tailed black cat was jumping up in the air. Les opened the little book and started flicking through the cartoons.

They were a black and white time capsule of Australia in the forties and fifties. All the men wore hats, the women looked frumpy and every snotty-nosed kid had a patch in his pants. There were no TV sets, the cars were all bombs and any references to money were in pounds, shillings and pence. But every cartoon was sketched with a laconic zaniness that had you laughing before you read the titles. And everywhere were these subtle references to gravy. Fried gravy, gravy on toast, gravy in aspic. Gravy Road. Gravy Town Hall. Post No Gravy. I think I see where Emile Mercier's coming from here, chuckled Les. A Frenchman, arriving in Australia in nineteen forty, used to eating beautiful garlic and wine sauces, would find it somewhat disconcerting to discover all we ate back then was food drowned with lumpy fuckin gravy. Especially a Frenchman with a sense of humour like he had. For a lowlife wog criminal, Bodene sure had his shit together for a good Australian movie. Les flicked through the other books of cartoons, drank some more vodka and had another look in the old green handbag.

There was nothing else. But on one side was a small zippered pocket. Les opened it up and inside was a frayed white hanky and knotted in the corner of the hanky were some coins. The knot had been tied for years. But Les was able to prise it open and take the coins out. There was a two-shilling piece, a sixpence and two pennies. Well, there you go, smiled Les. It wasn't such a prick of a day after all. I made three thousand, five hundred dollars, two shillings and eight pence. Or in today's currency, three thousand five hundred dollars and twenty-seven cents. Les raised his glass and laughed ironically.

'To Rose the tarot card lady,' he said. 'You were right. I did get my reward. And I did find something else that was old. You little beaut.'

Les replaced everything back in the bag and folded the coins up in the hanky. He sipped on his vodka and stared balefully into space, once again agreeing George Brennan had every right to tell him he had a pumpkin for a head, when the front door opened. Footsteps sounded in the hallway before Beatrice appeared in the loungeroom dressed in a pair of green slacks, a white shirt and a matching green vest. Her long black hair was shining and she had a smile on her face, which soon disappeared when she saw Les.

'Hey. Hello Beatrice,' smiled Les. 'How are you, mate?'

Beatrice studied Les from behind her glasses. 'My God, Les,' she said. 'What happened to you?'

'I got into a fight, Beatrice,' replied Les.

'Crikey. Who with? Anthony Mundine and his father?'

'No. Just some horrible punters. So how was the Gold Coast?'

'Not all that good,' smiled Beatrice. 'It rained. And Warren had a bad cold the whole time.'

'Where is he?' Les asked.

'Bringing his things out of the car.'

'Right,' nodded Les.

Beatrice sniffed the air and looked at Norton's glass. 'Are you drinking Dutch Chocolate Vodka?'

'I sure am,' replied Les.

'Can I have one?' asked Beatrice.

'Beatrice,' said Les. 'You don't have to ask if you can have a drink when you're round here. Just help yourself. You're part of the scene.'

'Yeah, I know but ...'

Beatrice went to the kitchen, got two glasses and ice and made two drinks the same as Les was having. She brought them into the loungeroom, kept one and placed the other on the bar.

'I made one for Warren,' she smiled as she sat down on a lounge chair. 'Otherwise he might get the shits and start beating me up.'

Les raised his glass. 'That's our Woz. He's a brute when it comes to women.'

The front door closed, more footsteps sounded in the hallway and Warren appeared in the loungeroom wearing a pair of jeans and a matching denim shirt. His hair was untidy and he looked somewhat tired and drawn.

'Hello, Woz,' greeted Les. 'How are you, mate?'

'Better than you, ugly,' replied Warren. 'Jesus Christ! What happened to your fuckin head?'

'Like I told Beatrice,' replied Les. 'I got into a fight.'

'I made you a drink, Warren,' said Beatrice. 'It's on the bar.'

'Thanks.' Warren picked up his drink, took a sip and sat down on a lounge chair facing Les. 'So what happened while I was away? Did you find the missing bag?' Warren spotted the green bag sitting on the coffee table. 'Is that it? Is that the bag?' he said excitedly. 'So you did find it. You're a genius.'

'Yes. I found it, Warren,' replied Les.

Warren sipped some more vodka. 'Did you have any outside help?' he enquired. 'Or did you do it all on your own?'

'No. I did it all on my own, Woz,' replied Les.

Warren looked at Les a little askance. 'Wow,' he said. 'There's no stopping you, is there?'

'No. There's not.'

'So I guess all you got to do now is pick up your fifty grand off Bodene.'

Les shook his head. 'There is no fifty grand, Warren. Bodene just got busted.'

'Is that what happened?' Warren turned to Beatrice then back to Les. 'We just drove past his pizza joint and there were cops everywhere.'

'That's what happened, Warren. Bodene's off to the pokey. And my fifty grand is going with him.'

Warren tossed back his head and laughed that hard he started to cough. 'So you went to all that trouble and got your head bashed in for nothing. You moron.'

'Warren,' chided Beatrice.

'Not quite nothing, Warren,' smiled Les. 'I ended up with two shillings and eight pence.'

'With what?' said Warren.

'Two shillings and eight pence. In fact this might interest you, Beatrice.' Les took the hanky out of the old green bag and unfolded the coins. 'There you are, Beatrice. A two shilling piece, a sixpence and two pennies.'

'Wow. How about that,' smiled Beatrice. She peered over at the old coins. 'Tell me the dates, Les,' she said. 'You never know. They might be worth something.'

'Righto.'

Les had a mouthful of vodka and with Warren watching him while Beatrice sipped her glass of vodka, Les started checking the coins.

'Okay,' said Les. 'A 1950 two shillings.'

'Two shillings, 1950,' said Beatrice. 'Mmmhh. Maybe ten dollars.'

'A 1947 sixpence.'

'Mmmhh,' Beatrice murmered again. 'Depending on the mint mark. About the same. If it's in good condition.'

'A 1942 penny.'

Beatrice shook her head. 'A dollar if you're lucky.'

'And a 1930 penny,' concluded Les.

Beatrice stared at Les. 'What did you just say?' she asked.

'A 1930 penny,' replied Les.

'Show me.' Beatrice reached over and took the coin out of Norton's hand. 'My God. You're right,' she said. 'This is a 1930 penny.'

Beatrice was examining the old coin and Les wasn't taking a great deal of interest when Warren sneezed violently.

'Gesundheit,' said Les.

'Yeah. Something like that,' rasped Warren, reaching for a hanky in the pocket of his jeans.

Suddenly a deafening silence descended on the loungeroom. Beatrice was staring at the old penny while Warren dabbed at his reddened nose with his hanky. In the middle of the silence, Les turned to Warren, and fixed him with an icy gaze.

'What did you just say, Warren?' Les asked him, very slowly and very distinctly.

'What did I just say?' replied Warren. 'What do you mean? What are you talking about?'

'You just sneezed, Warren,' Les said quietly. 'I said, Gesundheit. And you replied, Yeah. Something like that.'

'So?' replied Warren, nervously.

Norton's eyes were two narrow slits of loathing. 'Something like that,' he said. 'Something like that. Why you rotten little . . .'

Warren put his drink down and stood up. 'I don't know what the fuck you're on about, Les,' he said. 'If you ask me, you've been punched in the head too much.'

'Punched in the head too much,' echoed Les. 'The raspy voice. The Bondi markets. That old house. Those two drag queens from that fuckin soap ad. You underhanded little prick.' Les sucked in some air then placed his drink on the coffee table and lumbered to his feet like a monster rising from a slab in a Hammer horror film. 'You . . .'

'Now Les. Control yourself,' said Warren, quickly moving towards the hallway. 'You know what you're like when you get things fucked up.'

'Control myself,' snarled Les. 'I'll show you control myself. You cunt of a thing.'

Beatrice looked up at Norton, shaking her head in disbelief. 'Les,' she said. 'This is a 1930 penny.'

'It is?' replied Les. 'Well give it here.' Les snatched the coin back from Beatrice and glared at her. 'Did your grandmother ever have a saying, Beatrice? You can stick that where the monkey stuck the penny?'

'Yes,' nodded Beatrice. 'Yes she did, actually.'

'Good.' Les held the coin in front of Beatrice's face and gave her a crazed smile. 'Because guess where this is going.' Holding the old penny, Les raced off down the hallway towards the open door. 'Come here, Warren,' he howled. 'I got something for you — my friend.'